The Safe Place

by Tehila Peterseil

PITSPOPANY

NEW YORK ◆ JERUSALEM

The events and characters in this book are fictitious.

The situations the characters find themselves in, however,

are all too real.

DEDICATION

For the hundreds of thousands of Kinnerets around the world.

ACKNOWLEDGMENTS

There are many people who deserve credit for making this book possible. I want to express my thanks —

To Dr. Tirzah Houminer, for reviewing the manuscript and for her cogent comments.

To Yehudit Eizenstock, Michal Rosenberger, and Meira Rosenzweig for exemplifying for me what teaching special education is all about.

To those who taught me: Hugette Kottek, Leah Bacon, Zelda Rubin, Tzipora Mack, Tirza Speier, Dr. Esther Ranells, Hindy Flam, Adina Aretz, Rahamim Melamed-Cohen, Meira Rosenzweig, Dvorah Kieffer, Nechama Lev-Ari, Dr. Stanley Schneider, Professor Y. Kol Tov, Rabbi Meir Jakobovitz, Rabbi Yehudah Kupperman, and Zvi Breuer.

To those who encouraged me: Leora Petrover, Esther Farbstein, Yossi Lieber, and my friends, Adina Shapiro and Naomi London.

To those who helped this book see the light of day: Chaim Mazo of Pitspopany Press, who *always* made time, and Miriam Kresh for proofreading.

And to those of my colleagues who create a camaraderie that makes special education not only rewarding, but worker-friendly too: Michal Grossman, Michal Holstein, Racheli Patinkin, Rachel Toledano, Haguit Pemyenta, Moriya Komemy, Shouly Goldschmidt, Devorah Raziel, Geula Nisim, Navit Sa'ad, Michal Weissman, Pam Spolter, Chaya Phillipson, Yonah Shapira, Racquell Smotny, Vered Cruner, Yocheved Levanon, Rachel Applestein, Michal Lev, Karen Kraminer, Naomi Kleinshpiez, and Ronit Abu, and of course, Yael Nachum and Michal Zingerevitz.

On a more personal note, I want to thank the two Queen Esthers in my life, my grandmothers, Mrs. Esther Schreiber and Mrs. Esther Peterseil, for their support. Thanks also to my cousin, Hepsi Maidenbaum, for her honesty.

Finally, I want to thank my family.

My brothers, Gedalia, Shlomo, Nachum, and Yosef for always being ready to lend a hand or a kind word.

My sisters, Tiferet, Temima, Todahya, and Tanya, for acting as my own private cheerleading section, whenever I needed cheering up.

My mother, for her encouragement and her interest in this project. She read each chapter as I wrote it and served as a "resource room" of experience for this novel.

And my father, for his enthusiasm and his zeal. He taught me the meaning of "constructive criticism." Thank you, Abba.

FOREWORD

Almost all of us know someone who has a learning disability. Experts estimate that approximately 15% of American school-age children have some form of learning disability. In the vast majority of cases, these disabilities are not caught in the early stages of schooling, but — through parental and/or administrative neglect or ignorance — left to fester within the child until they become obstacles that the child feels incapable of overcoming.

Not all learning disabilities are as serious as the ones described in this book, but for the child who has problems learning, these disabilities often become a burden almost too heavy to bear. Over time, the child begins to develop a negative self-image, a feeling of being "dumb" or incapable of successfully interacting with his or her peers. This feeling of loneliness and ostracization, which many parents and teachers are quick to pick up on, must not be interpreted as simply something the child will outgrow, but rather, as a warning sign of something more serious.

Alternately, a child acting out in class, the "class clown", may be trying to mask feelings of ineptitude by bringing the teacher's focus away from his or her scholastic failures.

As professionals, we have learned that the solutions to the problems of learning disabilities are never simple. We must build up the child's feeling of self-worth. To do this we often have to remove the child from some of his or her classes, for extended periods of time, and place him in a resource room or special class where specially trained teachers can work with the child, teaching him not only what to study but how to study as well. Ultimately, our aim is to mainstream the child back into the classroom as a self-assured, productive and successful individual.

The book you are about to read, *The Safe Place*, puts the reader into the mind of a child with special learning problems and carries the reader through the somersaults and conniptions that such children as Kinneret, the heroine of this story, go through. At the same time, it brings into focus the success of the specially designed programs that help to integrate these children into the school system.

This is a story of pain. But, more important, it is also a story of hope. It is an ongoing drama that is being acted out in schools all over America. A drama which *The Safe Place* helps us to understand.

Judah Weller
Educational Director
P'TACH

PART I

Teach me, and I will hold my peace.

Cause me to understand wherein I have erred.

Job 6:24

Chapter 1

Night.

Kinneret felt her pulse throbbing, its frantic pounding echoing in her neck and head, as she raced along the pavement. The back of her left hand swiftly swiped at her forehead to remove the sweat.

Run! Run!

She reached a lawn with hedges, staying low so she would not be seen. They were after her again — two figures in the shadows. They were so quick. She knew she could not afford even one small mistake. Kinneret's fear turned to terror. She just had to make it, had to get there — to the safe place. She was conscious of skimming the grass ever so lightly, of willing her feet to move forward. She crouched and waited for a moment. The two figures were close. Even from a distance they seemed to tower over her.

She felt her breath coming hard. She tried to stop heaving. Quiet! she told herself. Quiet.

The safe place. Which way? Kinneret looked out into the darkness at the unfamiliar terrain.

Which way? Which way?

I don't know which way to run!

They're so close.

Kinneret looked far out into the darkness. Run as fast as you can. Don't stop! Find the safe place. Don't stop!

But they knew what she was thinking. And they were so quick. So close. She prepared to run.

The shadow closest to her lunged.

Kinneret sat straight up, breathing hard, and found herself on the floor two feet away from her bed. She looked around the dark room. The hall light was on. The blanket was all tangled around her, and she could feel the sweat trickling down the side of her eye, down to her cheek.

Kinneret got up and peered into her sister's crib. The baby was sleeping soundly. Then she softly walked out of her room and stood by the doorway of her brothers' room. She envied their restful sleep. She returned to her room, picked up her blanket, and lay down on her bed. A stab of fear ran through her as she pulled the blanket up to her chin.

"I hate it when I have that dream," she said aloud, comforted by the sound of her own voice. She lay there quietly for a long time, reliving the nightmare that still left her whole body trembling and exhausted.

Gradually, she fell asleep, dreamless.

Chapter 2

"Kinneret, wake up. It's already seven o'clock. You'll be late for school."

Kinneret opened her eyes to the sight of her mother standing over her bed. Mrs. Pfeiffer pulled up the shades. The sun attacked Kinneret, blinding her and making her head hurt. It was as though the rays of light were drilling holes into the side of her head.

"No, don't close your eyes," her mother ordered. "I've made your clothes ready. Micah and Meyer are already dressed. I'm going to wake Elana."

"My head hurts, Ima," Kinneret moaned.

Mrs. Pfeiffer looked sternly at her second oldest child, but her sternness soon turned to compassion. "You always say your head hurts in the morning. Come on, sweetheart," she cajoled, "you'll feel better after you've eaten breakfast. Get dressed."

Kinneret sat up and felt the pain in her temples. It enveloped the back of her head as well. She stumbled into the bathroom and splashed water on her face.

"Kinneret, hurry up! It's 7:15 already!" her mother shouted.

Slowly, trying to ignore her headache, Kinneret started getting dressed.

Kinneret still hadn't put on her shirt when her mother walked into her room at 7:27.

"Kinneret, what takes you so long?"

Mrs. Pfeiffer snatched the shirt and quickly pulled it over her nine-year-old's head.

"Bring your knapsack to the kitchen with you!" she ordered. Kinneret grabbed her knapsack and entered the kitchen. Her mother gave her a glass of orange juice, and the throbbing in her head ebbed a little.

Meyer, Micah and Elana were eating cornflakes at the kitchen table. Ahuva, the oldest, grabbed her lunch and ran out the front door.

"Eat some breakfast," Mrs. Pfeiffer told Kinneret.

"I can't," Kinneret pleaded. "I don't think I remember —"

"Then drink some more orange juice," her mother interrupted. "I'm sure you remember. We practiced it for hours last night. Your teacher will be very happy with you."

Mrs. Pfeiffer looked at her daughter and smiled. "But, just to be sure, let me hear them one more time, dear."

Kinneret shut her eyes, "Sivan, Iyar —"

"Kinneret, it's Nissan."

"That's what I said," Kinneret insisted.

"No, you said Sivan." Mrs. Pfeiffer sighed. "Never mind, try again."

Kinneret closed her eyes. "I can't concentrate. Meyer's chewing too loudly."

"Boy, you're so picky about everything," her eight-year-old brother retorted.

"Try and be quiet just for a minute," Mrs. Pfeiffer said.

Again, closing her eyes, Kinneret began. "Nissan, Iyar, Sivan, Tamuz..."

"That's great, Kinneret. You'll do fine."

"What if I say it wrong, or if I forget?"

"You won't forget." Mrs. Pfeiffer smiled as she hugged her daughter.

Kinneret's headache was almost completely gone, except for a feeling of slight pressure behind her eyes.

"Pack your lunch, Kinneret. Meyer, tie your shoes. Micah, your face is filthy."

"Ima, where is my barrette?" Kinneret asked.

"Wherever you put it last night," Mrs. Pfeiffer answered.

"I can't find it." Kinneret ran into the bathroom and checked in the cabinet. Then she ran into her room and then back to the kitchen.

"I'll make you a ponytail," her mother volunteered, seeing how tense Kinneret had become.

"I hate ponytails," Kinneret whined, but turned to let her mother gather her hair.

"Goodbye," Mrs. Pfeiffer said as she finished fixing her hair. She kissed Kinneret's cheek. "Have a good day," she added, handing Kinneret her coat.

Kinneret walked out and was just about to close the door when she heard her mother shout, "Kinneret! Your lunch!"

Kinneret dashed into the kitchen and was out the door with her lunch before her mother could say anything.

She walked to the foot of the lawn to wait for the bus.

Mrs. Pfeiffer parted the kitchen shades and watched the slumped shoulders of her dark-haired daughter as she shuffled down the driveway.

"If only I could make it easier for you, Kinneret," Mrs. Pfeiffer sighed, tears welling in her eyes.

Kinneret picked up a dry yellow leaf and put it into her pocket. She silently boarded the bus.

Kinneret walked heavily through the bus. The children were talking and playing, but no one seemed to notice her.

"Hi, Kinneret," a voice rang out.

"Hi, Paula," Kinneret answered. Paula was a sixth-grader who was friendly with Dalia, Kinneret's friend.

Kinneret sat near the back of the bus. It was the same seat she sat in every morning. She rested her head on the window and looked out. A first-grader sat down beside her, but she didn't notice. Her headache was completely gone, and the moving bus seemed to soothe her.

The driver picked up the last student and was heading toward the bridge. At the other end of the bridge lay the school. As the wheels of the bus touched the first plank of the bridge, the pounding demon inside Kinneret's head awoke.

Don't go to school today, Kinneret silently begged the bus driver. Have a flat tire or forget where it is. Yes, forget where it is, she prayed, wincing. Her *school-ache* had begun. Her head would throb steadily now until school ended. Hopefully, it would never reach the kind of pain she felt in the mornings, but the pain would be there, just below the surface, just strong enough to keep her from concentrating.

The children started piling out of the bus, babbling and screaming as they greeted each other.

Kinneret got off last, forcing her legs to move forward as she entered the classroom.

Chapter 3

Mrs. Enstein entered like a whirlwind as the bell rang.

The school-ache moved up a notch as Kinneret anticipated the teacher's first question of the day.

"Who is going to lead prayers today?" she said cheerfully.

Don't pick me, Kinneret thought. I won't be able to say the words out loud, and I won't know how much time to leave for the other girls to finish. I'll be too slow.

She tried to look as busy as she could, gazing intently at her Hebrew-English *siddur.*

"Devorah, why don't you lead us this morning?" Mrs. Enstein suggested.

"Modeh ani lefanecha..."

Kinneret followed the words but had no idea of their meaning. When she lost her place — which was often — she would look at one of the girls who sat near her to check what page they were on.

After they were done, the class automatically put their siddurim away.

"Take out your Chanukah notebooks," the teacher said. Kinneret placed her notebook and pencil case on her desk. Her school-ache was bearable now.

"Girls," Mrs. Enstein announced, "who can tell me what we light on Chanukah in order to remind us of the Chanukah miracle?"

All twenty-eight hands shot up. Mrs. Enstein surveyed the room. Her eyes immediately rested on Kinneret, whose hand was stretched up high.

Mrs. Enstein noticed a light in Kinneret's usually sad, gray eyes.

"Yes, Kinneret?"

Kinneret smiled. "It's a thing that has nine round things coming out of the beginning and you can light it with oil or candles, you light another one of them each day." Kinneret said it as one long sentence.

Mrs. Enstein looked at her watch. "Yes, Kinneret, I see that you know what it is. But what is it called?"

Kinneret's smile withered. She was keenly aware of the sound of someone sharpening her pencil in the third row. She forced herself to think. "It rhymes with Devorah, and I think it has an *N* in it," she finished desperately.

Someone behind her giggled.

"Can anyone help Kinneret?" Mrs. Enstein asked.

Twenty-seven hands shot up.

"Yes, Gila." She smiled at the small blonde girl, her favorite pupil.

"A menorah."

"Excellent," Mrs. Enstein exclaimed.

Kinneret looked down at her hands, feeling ashamed and humiliated.

I'm so stupid, she thought. Mrs. Enstein thinks I need help with easy things.

"The Greeks came into the Temple," the teacher said, "and they opened all the jars of oil needed to light the menorah. This made the oil impure and created a terrible problem. How would they light the menorah? The Maccabees looked everywhere for oil but all they found was one little pitcher of oil, enough to light the menorah for one day. But it would take eight days to make pure new oil. So God performed a miracle. Can anyone tell me what that miracle was?" Twenty-eight hands shot up.

"Yes, Sharon?"

"The oil lasted eight days."

"That's right," the teacher said.

Who didn't know that? Kinneret told herself.

"It was a miracle that the oil in the menorah lasted for eight days," the teacher repeated. "Now, class, the principal has asked us to make our own Chanukah menorahs during class time. The principal will take the menorahs and display them in the halls for everyone to see."

A cheer went up from the class.

Naturally, Kinneret cheered along with the others. But she didn't get it. Why was everyone happy? What was the joke?

What if you didn't have your own Chanukah menorah? What if your mother didn't let you bring it in during class time? And why did everyone have to bring a menorah from home for the principal? How would he light so many menorahs? And why light them in the halls?

So many questions. So much confusion.

Kinneret looked around her, at Dalia and Leah and Rivka, and felt a sadness wash over her. Why don't I understand what's happening around me? she thought.

Kinneret knew that the only way to keep afloat and avoid really big headaches was to blend in. Being like everyone else was the key. So Kinneret smiled her biggest smile.

"Now, girls, quiet down. Who can tell me what month Chanukah is in?" Mrs. Enstein continued.

Although Kinneret had no idea, she knitted her brows in deep thought, knowing that Mrs. Enstein was evaluating all the girls. Only when Kinneret was sure that her teacher would call on Melissa did she raise her hand.

"Kislev," Melissa answered eagerly.

"That's right," Mrs. Enstein nodded.

"The 25th of Kislev," Melissa added.

"Very good," Mrs. Enstein applauded, proud that Melissa remembered the details.

"Now, girls, when I call on you, please recite all the names of the months that you have memorized.

"Ilana."

Ilana cleared her throat then started. "Nissan, Iyar, Sivan, Tamuz..."

"Good job." Mrs. Enstein put a little check by Ilana's name. "Dalia."

"Nissan, Iyar...."

"That's fine, Dalia," Mrs. Enstein acknowledged, adding another check to her list.

Dalia flashed a warm smile in Kinneret's direction. Kinneret smiled back.

You'll do fine. You won't forget. Kinneret remembered her mother's comforting words.

"Mindy," Mrs. Enstein called.

Mindy lowered her head.

"Mindy?"

"I didn't do it," Mindy admitted in a barely audible voice.

Mrs. Enstein's mouth was pursed into a thin line. There was not a sound in the class.

"See me at recess," she said softly. "I want to send a note home to your mother. Esther," she called out.

"Nissan, Iyar, Sivan, Tamuz, Av, Elul, uh..." Esther couldn't remember the rest of the months.

"Go on, Esther, I know you know the rest of the months," Mrs. Enstein assured her. Esther squinted her eyes in concentration, but she couldn't remember.

"Elul," Mrs. Enstein prompted.

That was all Esther needed. "Elul, Tishrei, Cheshvan..." she continued.

"Fine, Esther. See, I knew you could do it. Now Sharon."

"Nissan, Iyar, Sivan..."

"Good. Kinneret?"

Kinneret looked at her teacher's smiling face. Her own face was taut with fear.

How did it start again? Nissan, Sivan, Nissan, Sivan?

Kinneret remained mute.

"Kinneret, it's your turn," the teacher said, her smile more strained now.

Nissan, that was it, Kinneret thought. But her mouth formed the word "Sivan."

"Kinneret, speak louder. Start again from Nissan." The smile had vanished from Mrs. Enstein's face.

"Nissan, Iyar, Sivan, Tamuz, Av," she whispered.

"Kinneret, I still can't hear you," the teacher said.

Kinneret said loudly, "Nissan, Iyar —" and stopped. She could not remember anymore. All she could hear was Dalia tapping her fingers on her desk and someone giggling from somewhere behind her. It was impossible to concentrate.

Seeing the confused look on Kinneret's face, Mrs. Enstein asked, "What's wrong, Kinneret?"

Kinneret's face flushed red. Didn't the teacher hear all the noise? How could anyone concentrate with so much going on?

Her school-ache suddenly exploded. There were pinpoints of pain stabbing her just behind her right eyeball. The hammering in her head hurt her ears.

"I can't hear you, Kinneret," the stern-faced teacher said.

Kinneret looked toward the door and a voice deep inside her screamed out in fear and frustration. *Ima! Save me, please come save me. Take me away. I can't anymore!*

"Kinneret, we're waiting," the teacher said impatiently.

Kinneret tried to look at the teacher, but the pain in her head made it hard for her to focus.

"I think you didn't study last night, Kinneret," Mrs. Rubenstein said accusingly. "Am I right?"

Kinneret shivered involuntarily. "I did study," she said, using all her energy to get the words past the pain.

"Then continue," demanded the teacher.

"I can't," she said, closing her eyes.

Mrs. Enstein was about to say something else, and then thought better of it. She gave Kinneret an icy stare and called on someone else.

But Kinneret was already miles away by then. She had summoned the bird. And the bird had come. Her mother might not answer her, and God might be too busy to pay attention to her, but the bird always came.

Kinneret felt herself being lifted on the back of the beautiful, glittering white eagle. It was so big and she was so small, she knew that no one could see her. Then she felt the bird's strong wings flapping as they rose towards the open sky, the wind beating down on her face. In a flash, they were over the ocean. At that moment, her school-ache all but disappeared.

The rustling of paper brought Kinneret back to the classroom. She looked to her left, toward the window, for a sign of the bird, wishing she knew how to make it stay.

"The office," Mrs. Enstein began, "has informed me that some girls have not brought in the pink medical slip you were supposed to hand in at the beginning of the year. The following girls must bring the slip in by tomorrow."

"Ilana, Sharon, Miranda, Ahuva, Cynthia, Kinneret, Mindy, Rivka."

Kinneret's hand shot up as soon as she heard her name. But when she saw that no one else had their hand up, she quickly lowered her own. What was happening? She knew she was supposed to do something. Her eyes were opened wide. Was she suppose to go somewhere? Say something?

No one was moving yet, so, so far it was okay. She hoped she wasn't supposed to do anything, at least not until recess. At recess she would ask Dalia.

Kinneret waited impatiently for class to finish. She hated having to do something but not knowing what it was.

"Why did the teacher call my name?" Kinneret whispered to Dalia as they lined up in pairs for recess.

"Because you didn't bring the pink medical slip to the office," Dalia whispered back. "Don't forget to bring it tomorrow."

Kinneret nodded. "I brought some potato chips for us," she told her friend.

Dalia smiled. "I love potato chips."

Kinneret knew that.

She also knew she could not survive school without Dalia. What if one day Dalia got tired of explaining things to her?

"This afternoon we have a spelling bee in English," Dalia said excitedly.

"Yeah, well, you're good at spelling."

"Hey, Dalia, want to hear a joke?" Ahuva shouted out as they headed for the playground.

"Sure," Dalia yelled back, walking toward Ahuva.

"A patient came to his doctor and said, 'Doctor, doctor, everyone is ignoring me!' And the doctor said, 'Next patient, please!' "

All the girls around her started laughing. Kinneret laughed, too.

Why didn't the doctor answer him? Kinneret wondered. What was so funny about a doctor ignoring his patient?

The first, second, and third-grade girls were already on the playground by the time the fourth grade arrived. Rivka was holding the class ball.

"Let's play dodge ball!" Gila shouted.

"Yeah!" shouted most of the girls.

"They always say yes to whatever Gila says," Kinneret complained to Dalia. "Let's go play in the playground."

"No, let's play dodge ball with the class," Dalia coaxed. "Come on, I need you."

"I hate dodge ball," Kinneret said, dryly.

"Oh, come on, you're great at dodge ball. You throw the ball so hard that no one can catch it. You always get almost everyone out."

"I don't like the way they play. It's...too...too...too...political," Kinneret blurted out.

"Where did you learn that word?" Dalia asked, amused.

"I don't know," Kinneret mumbled. "But it's true."

"Oh come on! Who'll pass me the ball? Please! I *need* you."

Kinneret looked at Dalia, realizing she owed her friend too much to refuse such a simple request. But she sensed there would be trouble. "Okay," she sighed.

Kinneret was right. The fourth-graders passed the ball to their friends, which meant that outsiders like Kinneret were at a disadvantage. But Kinneret had one thing that almost evened the odds: speed.

Rivka threw the ball up in the air.

The girls scattered.

Four girls ran for the ball. Kinneret wasn't one of them. You never knew where the ball would land, and Kinneret, despite her speed, was worried someone else would get the ball first.

Melissa scooped up the ball as Mindy braked and started running away. In one swift motion, Melissa heaved the ball at Mindy's back. She missed. Daniella grabbed the ball and aimed at Aliza, hitting her smack on her hip. She was out.

Kinneret stayed away from the center, biding her time until the ball came her way. She hated the idea of people getting out. Why couldn't everyone stay in and play? she wondered. Nevertheless, Kinneret knew that playing was better than being out. Being out meant you weren't good enough. And anyway, Dalia was depending on her.

Aliza started yelling, "Get Daniella out!" from the sidelines. Gayla darted for the ball and aimed at Daniella. She missed. Then Mindy got the ball and passed it to Ilana, who aimed at Sharon. She was standing ten feet away. It hit Sharon on her arm, and Sharon was out, too. The class understood that Mindy and Ilana were going to help each other. Everyone would try to stay away from both of them now.

Kinneret saw her chance and, utilizing her speed, raced Gila, Marsha, and Debra for the ball. She caught the ball and prepared to throw it. But instead of trying to hit the girls around her, she bounced the ball to Dalia.

"Hey, no passing on a bounce!" Gila shouted.

"Mindy passed," Aliza pointed out.

"I didn't bounce it!" Mindy yelled.

"What's the difference?" Kinneret asked, not understanding the fine points of the game.

"Passing on a bounce slows down the game, and it's too easy to catch," Mindy informed her, talking to Kinneret like she would to a baby.

"I don't care," Dalia said, seeing that this could lead to trouble. "Take the ball."

"No!" Kinneret insisted fiercely. "It's your ball!"

"You're such a cheater, Kinneret," Gila accused.

"Let's just play," interrupted Sharon.

"Yeah, let's play," agreed Gayla and Miranda.

The girls returned to their positions and soon forgot about the argument.

I am *not* a cheater, Kinneret thought indignantly.

Dalia threw the ball up high. Sara caught it.

"Get Rena!" Dalia shouted.

Sara aimed at Rena and hit her between the shoulder blades. Kinneret scooped up the ball and threw it at Sara, but she missed her by a good two feet. Naomi grabbed the ball and aimed at Gila, who stood fifteen feet away. Bang! She hit her on the calf, almost knocking her over.

"You're out!" Naomi shouted, elated at having successfully ousted Gila from the game.

"It missed," Gila insisted.

"It hit your foot!" Kinneret stated.

"It hit the floor!" Gila hissed.

"You're out!" Kinneret insisted.

"It hit you," a few of the girls mumbled in agreement.

"You weren't standing near me. You didn't see!" Gila yelled back at them. "You're all such cheaters, and Kinneret is the biggest cheater of all!"

Kinneret turned to her classmates, who were clearly ready to give in to Gila. "Why are you all so scared of her? Why don't you tell her the truth?" she demanded.

"Oh, go buy yourself a brain, loser," Gila lashed out.

Kinneret's eyes betrayed the deep pain she felt as Gila's words hit their mark. Gila always knew where to strike. Kinneret was learning, the hard way, why the girls wouldn't stand up to her.

"And you're so — oh, never mind," Kinneret said, angry with herself for being unable to find an appropriate description. *If only I could think on my feet,* she thought.

"Don't let what she says get to you," Dalia said, in an effort to comfort her friend.

"I don't care what SHE says," Kinneret lied, trying to control the anger in her voice.

"Let's stop playing and go to the playground," Dalia suggested.

Kinneret's eyes narrowed. "No! I want to finish this game," she announced ominously.

The game continued.

This time Kinneret played with a new found zeal. She took chances and ran frantically for every ball within fifteen feet of her. Although she managed to catch the ball most of the time, her anger clouded her aim, and she missed Gila time after time.

"Stop it, Kinneret!" Gila demanded as the ball whizzed by her. By now, almost fifty percent of all the throws were being thrown by Kinneret at Gila. Gila was beginning to feel the effects of trying to outrace Kinneret's anger. She was breathing heavily and, except for the fact that she didn't want to give the others the satisfaction of watching her leave, Gila would have gladly sat out the rest of the game.

Kinneret ignored her. Nor did she say anything when Gila stuck out her foot and "accidentally" tripped her. She felt no pain, although both her knees were bruised.

She was sweating, and her face was red, yet Kinneret felt cold. She kept running and throwing the ball like a robot.

Sharon picked up the ball and aimed at Miranda but missed. Although Gila was closer to the ball than she was, Kinneret managed to scoop up the ball the second it bounced. As soon as Gila realized Kinneret had the ball again, she turned to run. But it was too late. At at this distance, even a blind person would have been able to hit her.

Kinneret grabbed the ball with both hands and, with a *whoosh* as she exhaled, slammed the ball into Gila's back.

"You're out!" Kinneret declared emphatically as Gila flew forward. The ball, like a backpack, seemed stuck to her back. She hit the ground with a thud. Her screams pierced the sudden quiet that had settled among the players. Gila had blood on both her hands and knees.

"You're going to be in big trouble," Gila bawled as some of the girls came to help her up. Just then, the bell rang, signaling the end of recess.

The girls went back to their classroom. Gila was being helped by two girls who had offered to take her to the nurse.

"Kinneret, you shouldn't get so upset. She wasn't worth the trouble you're going to get into," Dalia said.

"It's not right. None of it isn't right," Kinneret raged, with a nine-year-old's sense of justice.

Dalia was about to comment on Kinneret's odd grammar structure but, seeing the anger in Kinneret's eyes, thought better of it.

Chapter 4

The fourth grade filed into their classroom and went to their seats. Kinneret sat down, her face feeling red-hot. Mrs. Flaumen walked in, smiling at the class.

"Today we're going to actually perform the science project we talked about last week," Mrs. Flaumen said excitedly.

Mrs. Flaumen walked over to Kinneret and placed her arm on her shoulder. Kinneret took a deep breath and smiled. The teacher returned the smile.

"Remember what we learned last week?"

Kinneret nodded, feeling self-conscious, yet trying to reconstruct the last lesson. She looked at the items on the teacher's desk. There were a bunch of metal wires, a battery, and a lightbulb.

What is this? Kinneret wondered.

"I have a question for you," Mrs. Flaumen said to Kinneret.

Kinneret's shoulders stiffened. Mrs. Flaumen, her hand still resting on those shoulders, didn't seem to notice.

"Look at the lightbulb, Kinneret, and tell me whether the circuit is open or closed."

Please take your hand off me, Kinneret begged silently. I can't call the bird if you touch me.

"Kinneret?"

Kinneret looked at the lightbulb. It was lit. She relaxed. "It's open," she said confidently, looking up at her teacher's face.

"Are you sure, Kinneret?"

Kinneret knew she had said the wrong thing. But the light was on! It was open!

"Ahuva, can you repeat the law about the electric circuit?"

"When the circuit's wires are open, the lightbulb isn't connected to the electricity and the light is closed. When the circuit's wires are closed and connected to the bulb, the light is open," Ahuva quoted from memory.

"Very good! I see you remembered," Mrs. Flaumen said, smiling.

"Kinneret, now can you tell me the law of the electric circuit?" Mrs. Flaumen asked encouragingly.

Kinneret looked into her teacher's kind eyes.

"The circuit's wire...the bulb isn't together...electricity and the light is closed...the circuit...and, and then it's, uh, open," Kinneret babbled, trying to sound confident. It was all she could remember.

Mrs. Flaumen continued to smile. "I see it's hard for you to express yourself, but I think you understand."

I don't! Kinneret thought.

"Now, Kinneret, look at the lightbulb. Is the circuit open or closed?"

Kinneret looked at the bulb. It was out now.

She took a deep breath. "It's closed," she said. But after a quick look at her teacher's face, she blurted out, "I mean open."

"That's right," Mrs. Flaumen said. "Now again."

The bulb was lit.

Kinneret tried to think. When I say open, the answer is closed; when I say closed, the answer is open. This is so frustrating.

THEY KEEP CHANGING THE RULES! she silently screamed.

Open means closed, and closed means open. How can I remember all the words when they keep changing their meaning?

She looked at the lightbulb, at the light, and said sadly, "It's closed."

"That's good," Mrs. Flaumen clucked.

"Esther, your turn. Is the circuit open or closed?"

Kinneret looked at the light which was on.

"Closed," Esther said, smiling.

How does everyone know beforehand when the meanings of words change? Kinneret wondered. She placed her elbows on her desk and cupped her chin in both hands. Then she looked out toward the ocean. "At least the ocean never changes," she mumbled to herself.

The bell rang.

"Yes! Library Hour!" Melissa screamed.

"It's not for an hour. It's only for twenty minutes." Sharon said.

"Yes, but it's still called 'Library Hour,' " Miranda pointed out.

Mrs. Bluestein entered the room with a pile of books in her arms. She looked like she was seventy years old to the girls, although she was only fifty-four. Her face was very wrinkled, but her eyes were sapphire blue. They sparkled. She was barely five feet tall.

"Hello, girls. How is school?" she asked as she did every week.

"Amelia Bedelia, Amelia Bedelia!" the girls cried out.

"Amelia Bedelia it will be," Mrs. Bluestein announced, her thin lips parting in a smile. "Last week we started *GOOD WORK AMELIA BEDELIA*. Who can tell me where we left off?"

Fifteen hands shot up, including Kinneret's.

"Yes, Rivka?"

"We learned that Mr. Rogers wanted to eat breakfast, and he wanted toast and an egg, and Amelia Bedelia the housekeeper gave him a raw egg, and he was angry, so he said, 'Go fly a kite,' and she did." Everyone laughed.

"Wonderful," Mrs. Bluestein bubbled. "Who can go on from there? Arielle?"

Arielle thought for a moment and then began. "And then, so, Amelia Bedelia came back, then Mr. and Mrs. Rogers gave her a list of things to do. She did everything in a strange way; she raised the bread on a string so it should rise, and she cleaned the fireplace. She filled the wood box with the ashes instead of with wood and...that's all."

"Very well done, Arielle. What do you think will happen when Mr. and Mrs. Rogers come home? Rena?"

"They'll be angry."

"Why, Rena?"

"Because Amelia Bedelia did everything all wrong, and nothing will be ready."

"How will Amelia Bedelia feel? Kinneret."

"Bad. Amelia Bedelia will feel bad and sad."

"Why, Kinneret?"

"Because she's all mixed up. And every time she wants to do something, she does it wrong and everybody's angry, and she wanted so much to help and..." Kinneret couldn't go on. She felt too much of herself coming through. For a moment her school-ache threatened to reappear.

"That's good, Kinneret," Mrs. Bluestein said. "You're very perceptive."

Kinneret wasn't sure what "perceptive" meant, but she realized the teacher had complimented her. Her school-ache disappeared as quickly as it had come. Kinneret was very happy that there was such a thing as Library Hour.

"All right, girls. I'm continuing to read from page 20."

"That's done," said Amelia Bedelia. "What's next? Pot the window-box plants. Put the pots in the parlor." Amelia Bedelia went outside. She counted the plants, then she went into the kitchen.

"My goodness," she said, "I need every pot for this." So she took them all. Amelia Bedelia potted those plants, and she took them inside.

The girls laughed. Only Kinneret did not join them. She thought, poor Amelia Bedelia, poor Amelia Bedelia.

Mrs. Bluestein turned the page just as Miss Platkin started flute practice with the fifth-grade class next door.

"Don't worry, girls. We'll hear the story with the music. It'll make it more dramatic."

But Kinneret did not find "Three Blind Mice" dramatic. She only found it annoying. Terribly, terribly annoying. Concentrate on the story, she told herself as Mrs. Bluestein resumed reading.

"Three blind mice, Three blind mice..."

The NOISE! Miss Platkin screaming at her students. Mrs. Bluestein reading. The flutes fifing in the background.

Kinneret tried to concentrate, but it was no use. Instead, she closed her mind to everything and looked out toward the unchanging ocean. She didn't hear Mrs. Bluestein announce lunch. She got up from her chair only after she noticed the girls scrambling for their lunch boxes.

In the lunchroom, Kinneret sat down next to Dalia. The pandemonium created by dozens of girls talking at once always made her nervous. Kinneret washed, and ate her peanut butter and jelly sandwich. Martin Schwartz, the new student-teacher in the school, entered the lunchroom and stood up on a small podium that was in the center of the lunchroom. The one hundred and fifty voices of the first through sixth-grade classes gradually quieted down.

"All right girls," Martin announced, "which of you can come up here and say the Hebrew alphabet backwards?"

Only seven girls raised their hands.

"Batsheva from the third grade, come on up here."

He sounds like a talk show host, Kinneret thought.

Batsheva, smiling good naturedly, stood on the podium with Martin. She put her finger to her lips.

"Taf sin , shin uh...uh...uh wait!" She started whispering the aleph-bet forward to herself. "Resh!" she screamed out, then started once again from the beginning.

"That's enough Batsheva. Thank you very much," Martin said, and gave her a big red gumball that she popped into her mouth as she ran, giggling, to her friends.

"I don't want to embarrass anyone, so I'll show you how to do it."

Martin turned his back to the girls and started reciting "Aleph bet gimmel dalet heh.." Then he turned around. "Get it, girls? I'm standing backwards, with my back to you, and reciting the aleph-bet."

Kinneret didn't get it.

The younger girls laughed. Some of the older girls snickered.

"Now who wants to recite the aleph-bet backwards?" Martin announced again. "This is easy, girls."

Shira rolled her eyes at Dalia.

"What are we supposed to do?" Kinneret whispered to Dalia.

"Just stand up with your back to the girls and say the aleph-bet forwards."

But didn't he say backwards? Kinneret wondered to herself.

How can forwards be backwards and backwards be forwards? They're changing the rules again. Why?

Why?

The two girls joined the other fourth-graders, who left the lunchroom, guided by their English teacher, Mrs. Braun.

"Come on, Kinneret," Dalia coaxed. "Now's the good part. English, and then before you know it, we'll be going home."

"We only go home at four o'clock. That's a long time," Kinneret explained.

"But we have the spelling bee today."

"Don't remind me," Kinneret sighed as they entered the classroom.

"Girls. Sit, please," Mrs. Braun said dryly. "Today we're going to start off with the spelling bee I promised. I want you to listen carefully. Half of you will line up on the right side of the room, near the windows. The other half will line up on the left side of the room, by the coat rack. I will say a word, you will repeat it, spell it, and repeat it again. Okay, girls, line up."

Kinneret ran to stand near a window so she could view the ocean. Then she turned to watch the stampede of girls fighting to be first in line. The words in the beginning were easiest, so most of the girls wanted to be up front. It wasn't a problem for Kinneret to slip in last.

Kinneret held the class record for getting out on the first word. Her big fear was to be the first one to sit down. By being last in line, she stood a good chance that someone else would get out first.

"First word: 'fire'," the teacher announced.

Gila, who was first on the other line, repeated, "Fire, f-i-r-e, fire."

"That's right," Mrs. Braun said.

Gila took her place at the end of her line.

Mrs. Braun turned to the girls near the window. "Children," she said.

"Children," Debra, the first girl on line, echoed. "C-h-i-l-d-r-e-n, children."

"That's correct."

Debra smiled and went to stand behind Kinneret. Kinneret watched as girl after girl answered correctly. No one had even hesitated. Slowly, Kinneret inched forward, wishing the line would freeze.

"Engine," Mrs. Braun said to Melissa.

"Engine," Melissa repeated. "E-n—" She stopped. Her mind had gone blank on her.

Get out. Don't make it, Kinneret prayed, knowing it was wrong, but unable to control herself.

"E-n-g-i-n-e, engine," Melissa blurted, in one breath.

"That's correct." Mrs. Braun turned to Esther, the last girl on line on the other side.

"Surprise," she said.

"Surprise," Esther repeated.

Don't make it! Don't make it! Kinneret wished with all her might. The school-ache was starting, and she could feel the pain behind her eyes.

"S-e-r-p-r-i-s-e, surprise?" Esther said, uncertainly.

"I'm sorry. That is incorrect," the teacher told her.

Esther half-smiled, then shrugged her shoulders, and went to sit down in her seat. She took out her crayons and some paper and started coloring.

Kinneret watched Esther sit down.

I'm sorry, Esther, she wanted to scream. You're out because of me. It's my fault. I'm so mean. But she had little time for pity. Her turn was next, and her head was hurting badly.

Mrs. Braun took a look at Kinneret, who was next in line.

She looked at the child standing before her with clenched fists, nervously biting her lower lip. She silently turned to the beginning of the list to find an easy word.

"Beach," she said.

"Peach," Kinneret whispered.

"The word is 'beach', Kinneret. Look outside, we're looking at the beach."

"Beach," Kinneret began again, embarrassed. She saw the spelling in her head: b-e-a-c-h. If only she could say it.

Kinneret felt cold. "B-e..." what was that letter called?

The one in the beginning of the alphabet. *A* — that was it.

"B-e-a..."

The class was quiet, too quiet. It made Kinneret feel self-conscious and unsure.

Is the next letter called *C* or *S?* Oh yes, the beach is like the sea. That's an *S* sound.

"B-e-a-s-h. Beach," Kinneret sputtered.

I got it right! she thought ecstatically, and looked sadly over at Esther who was coloring away.

"I'm sorry, that is incorrect."

Kinneret stared at her teacher, dumfounded.

But I said it right, she thought.

"Please sit down, Kinneret," the teacher commanded. Kinneret walked to her seat. Twenty-seven pairs of eyes followed her as she slid into her chair.

She looked toward the ocean. Outside it was drizzling. She noticed that the grayness of the sky and sea matched almost perfectly. The gray-black storm clouds were billowing, rolling over the entire horizon. Kinneret saw the playground getting wet, then watched the rain-drops hit the water.

"When do you stop being raindrops and start being part of the ocean?" Kinneret whispered to the rain.

"Girls," Mrs. Braun announced, "only Gila and Dalia are left. Let's see who will be the spelling-bee champ of the class."

"Rhyme," the teacher called out.

"Rhyme," Gila repeated. "R-h-y-m-e, rhyme."

"That is correct," the teacher said. "Now, Dalia, please spell the word 'restaurant'."

"Restaurant," Dalia repeated, "R-e-s-t-a-u-r-a-n-t, restaurant."

"That is correct. And for you, Gila, we have the word 'satellite'."

"Satellite," Gila repeated, "s-a-t-e-l-i-t-e, satellite."

"I am sorry, that is incorrect."

Gila's face fell.

"Dalia, can you spell satellite?" the teacher asked.

"Satellite, s-a-t-e-l-l-i-t-e, satellite."

"That is correct. Dalia is the class spelling-bee champ," Mrs. Braun announced. The class applauded. Kinneret clapped the loudest.

"All right, girls," the teacher said, opening a folder marked *math*. "Take out your math books. I'll be returning your math tests today."

Kinneret took out her math book and waited for her test.

"Nina, come take your test. Gayla, Melissa, Laura, Sharon, Debra." Each of the girls went up to the teacher's desk to receive her test. "Kinneret, Aliza, Rena."

Kinneret walked over to her teacher, took the test, and smiled. Strangely, her teacher did not smile back.

I know I did well. I studied hard for this test, Kinneret thought confidently as she took the folded paper. She waited until she sat down to look at her grade.

It was the redness of the page that shocked her at first.

All the numbers I worked on and wrote down so carefully are ruined. So many *x*'s. And I only got 15%. How could that be?

Kinneret placed her elbows on her desk and put her cheeks between her hands. She tried not to cry, but her lips began to tremble.

Why did she write that I'm care*less*? I'm not careless. I care a lot.

A wave of sadness passed over her as she realized, I can't do better. Why does she write that I can? Everyone keeps saying I can do better. Better than what? Better than I can do? But I'm doing what I can do! I can't help it if it always comes out all wrong.

Dalia slipped over to Kinneret before Mrs. Braun finished handing out the test papers.

"Kinneret?" she whispered.

Kinneret looked up. She had transformed herself. A bright smile appeared where her lips had trembled before. She quickly covered her paper.

"Whadya get?" Dalia asked innocently.

"Oh, just an eighty," Kinneret lied, trying to sound nonchalant. She deftly put her test paper into her knapsack.

"Hey, that's pretty good," Dalia said, proud of her friend. "I got an eighty-seven."

Kinneret smiled again. "That's great!" Kinneret said as Dalia returned to her seat.

It's so hard to smile when you're crying inside, Kinneret thought.

"Girls, turn to page 24 in your workbooks and calculate all ten equations," Mrs. Braun told the class when she finished handing out the tests. She walked over to Kinneret's desk and bent down so that she was eye to eye with Kinneret.

"Kinneret, I'm going to ask Aviva to go over the clock with you.

She'll help you learn it. Okay?"

Kinneret nodded, because she was afraid not to.

Aviva and Kinneret went to the back of the classroom.

Aviva picked up the cardboard clock.

"Okay, these are the numbers," Aviva began. "The little hand is the hour, and the big hand is the minutes. Now, if I put the little hand on the four, like this, and the big hand on the twelve, what time is it?"

Kinneret thought hard, not wanting to appear dumb.

"It's four o'clock," Aviva explained, wondering how anyone would not know that. "So if I put the little hand on the six, what time is it?"

"Six o'clock," Kinneret answered at once.

"Great. And if I put the little hand on the seven?"

Kinneret's face brightened. "Then it's seven o'clock."

"Right."

Kinneret started to relax.

"Now, what will happen if I put the little hand on the seven and the big hand here on the four?"

"It will be 7:04."

"No, it will be —"

"Oh, I know! It will be seven-forty," Kinneret interjected.

"No. The four in minutes is twenty."

Kinneret looked blankly at Aviva. She was tempted to laugh. "But four is four. If the big hand goes on the four it's four, so why should it be twenty when the little hand goes on it?"

"That's what it is," Aviva insisted.

Kinneret was beginning to get frustrated. "But how am I supposed to know that?"

"You remember," Aviva replied, getting frustrated herself.

"Okay, four is twenty."

"Yeah, and three is fifteen."

"Okay." Kinneret was ready to agree to anything, since it seemed so arbitrary anyway.

Thinking Kinneret actually understood the concept, Aviva went on. "And another way to say fifteen is a quarter, so when the big hand is on the fifteen and the little hand is on the eight, for example, you say eight and a quarter."

"How can that be? A quarter means twenty-five," Kinneret told her.

"No it doesn't. A quarter is fifteen."

Kinneret thought about the quarters her father gave her. He had always told her that a quarter was twenty-five cents. Could he have been wrong?

"No, Aviva. I'm sure a quarter means twenty-five," Kinneret maintained.

Aviva started getting angry. "But on a clock it's fifteen. You want to ask the teacher?"

"No," Kinneret replied quickly.

"Okay, so we got that a quarter is fifteen?"

"Yes," Kinneret answered, feeling the school-ache slowly enfold her head. They changed the rules again! The mute, frustrated voice cried out from inside her. Every time I learn a new rule they change it!

A few minutes later, Mrs. Braun approached them.

"It's time to stop. How did it go?"

"Aviva's a great teacher," Kinneret said quickly.

Aviva had been ready to tell the teacher how hard it had been, but instead she beamed.

"I knew you would be," Mrs. Braun smiled. "All you need to be a teacher is patience and understanding. Since you girls did so well together, you can do this again tomorrow."

Oh no, Kinneret thought.

"Both of you can sit down now and do the word problems on page 24."

Kinneret shuffled to her seat and opened her workbook.

Three men went to buy potatoes.
Ben bought 26 potatoes.
Eric bought 42 potatoes more than Ben.
Michael bought 36 potatoes less than Ben and Eric together.
How many potatoes did each man buy?

Kinneret read the question again.

What am I supposed to do first? There are so many words. How am I supposed to write it? Is the word problem plus or minus? Once it says more, and then it says less.

Kinneret sat down, feeling overwhelmed by the question in front of her, and didn't write a thing in her workbook.

"Girls, how many of you have finished?" Mrs. Braun asked.

Twenty girls raised their hands.

"Are the rest of you almost finished?"

Most of the girls nodded their heads.

Kinneret stared at her blank paper, wondering if maybe everyone was lying. How could they possibly know what to write?

Five minutes later, Mrs. Braun declared, "All right girls, whoever hasn't finished should do it for homework."

It's not fair, Kinneret thought. I always come home with the most homework and it's so hard. When will it end?

She sighed and closed her eyes.

Then the bird came.

It looked big and white and radiant. In an instant, she felt herself on its back. With her fingers around its neck, feeling its softness against her knees, nothing else mattered. The bird took her over the sea in between the raindrops. She could see the dark gray sea now. It was looming and vast and beautiful. Here was something no one else in the class knew or even imagined — the beauty of the dark, brooding sea.

The question "Does anyone have anything to say before we go out for recess?" melted her daydream.

"I have a complaint!" a voice Kinneret recognized only too well declared from the back of the room.

Kinneret turned her head toward that voice. A red sign flashed in her head. "DANGER."

Gila.

"At recess, when we were playing dodge ball, Kinneret called me a name," Gila wailed, "and then she kept wanting to get me out. She kept throwing the ball hard at me on purpose, and then at the end of the game she slammed it into my back and I fell, and I was bleeding, and she was happy," Gila sniffled, trying to catch her breath. She had told the entire tale in one breath.

Mrs. Braun turned angrily toward Kinneret. Twenty-seven faces turned toward her as well. You could hear a pin drop.

"Kinneret, what do you have to say?"

"I didn't," Kinneret said softly, feeling doomed, still thinking about the first part of Gila's complaint. She hadn't called her a name. At least she thought she hadn't.

"It seems to me like you did something," Mrs. Braun said accusingly.

Kinneret furrowed her brows, and a look of pure pain was etched on her face.

Everyone is against me, she thought silently. All her feelings welled up inside her and were caught at the back at her throat. She couldn't think of a word to say. It was as though she were wordless, language-less.

She wanted to tell her teacher about the things Gila had said and done. But even if she had been able to speak, she wouldn't have. The pain in her head was excruciating. The hammers were pounding, and their sounds overpowered any sound she could possibly make.

Mrs. Braun took Kinneret's silence as a sign of guilt. She was angry at this child, who took up so much of her time, who bullied girls smaller than her.

"Now look here, Miss," Mrs. Braun said, her voice rising steadily with each word. "I do not allow violence in my class. I will not have you picking on the other children. Do you hear me?"

Kinneret didn't really hear Mrs. Braun. She just kept telling herself, I will not cry. I will not cry, over and over again.

"I am very disappointed and angry with you, Kinneret. You may not leave your seat during recess." Then, turning to the class, the teacher said, "Except for Kinneret, you may all get up now. But no one go outside. It's raining."

REVENGE! Kinneret thought. One day I'll do something great and you'll all be sorry. One day I'll be smart and powerful and then I'll pretend I don't know you.

Then the bird came.

Kinneret felt herself being swiftly lifted onto its back. She was out of the school building, over the angry ocean. It was okay now. He was taking her far, far away to a place that was kind and fair. She felt the rushing of the wind against her face. She was over the ocean, flying high.

"Hey, honey." An unfamiliar voice shattered her reverie. She looked around her, momentarily seeking out the bird, but it was gone. She felt disappointed.

"Can you hand me the pliers?" the voice said.

Kinneret saw a ladder behind her. She looked up, and saw a middle-aged woman in blue overalls pulling out wires where one of the lightbulbs used to be.

She looked around her, seeing her friends trading stickers and playing jacks.

Kinneret looked down at the tools spread out on a towel on the floor. Which is the pliers? she wondered.

She picked up one of the tools.

"The one next to that one," the woman instructed gently.

Hesitantly, Kinneret picked it up and reached up to hand it to her.

"Thank you, hon. I see you're a dependable one." The woman smiled good-naturedly at Kinneret.

Kinneret looked at her, overcome, unable to smile back. She wanted to cry out in sheer gratitude because the woman had been nice to her; had even given her a compliment!

"Girls, find your seats. Recess is over," Mrs. Braun announced.

The girls reluctantly sat down. Kinneret felt a strong urge to move, to jump and run. She started shaking her legs.

"Take out your grammar books," the teacher said. "Kinneret, please tell the class the last grammar rule we learned in class."

Kinneret sensed that the teacher expected her not to know the answer. Mrs. Braun expected her to make up some excuse, or to look down at her desk, or, worse yet, to look blankly at her. She knew the teacher thought she was stupid, and lazy. The more Kinneret thought about it, the more she was determined to prove the teacher wrong. With a tremendous effort, she managed to control the pounding in her head and, taking a deep breath, recited, "When count nouns take a plural form, *S* is added."

The teacher had already formed the word "no" with her mouth, anticipating Kinneret's inability to answer. She blinked twice and then said, "Why, that's right, Kinneret. Yes. You see that you do know. Now, try and listen." For the first time, Mrs. Braun actually *believed* that Kinneret might actually be a good student if she tried and listened. But she had no idea how to make her try or how to get her to listen.

Kinneret was happy, if only for a moment. She had answered correctly and saw from the teacher's dazed expression that she had won this battle. Mrs. Braun would think twice next time before thinking that she was stupid.

But Kinneret's joy was short-lived. I don't know it, the mute, angry voice was saying inside. I only remember the words. I don't know what they mean. 'When count nouns take a plural form'. What are 'count nouns'? How do you 'count' them? What does it all mean?"

What a funny world this is, Kinneret thought, thinking about what she had learned this day. Everyone tells me I understand when I really don't, and then they tell me I don't understand when I really do. How do they know what I understand if I don't know myself?

It was five minutes to four. Mrs. Braun was getting ready to dismiss the class.

"Girls, put your coats on and zipper up. It's cold outside. I want you to go straight to your buses."

The girls stood up to put on their coats. Kinneret was happy just to be allowed to stand up. She stretched her legs, feeling relieved. The day was over, and she was going home.

Mrs. Braun led the class downstairs and pushed open the heavy school-building door. She said goodbye to her students as they ran out to board the already-waiting yellow school buses.

Kinneret walked out and felt the first gust of wind biting at her face. She wanted to yell out, "Freedom!" but instead, pulled back her hood and let the flood of rain drench her head. She ran toward the boardwalk and faced the ocean. She stared at the raging, roaring ocean, toward the black, angry clouds and the thunder, feeling the freezing raindrops cruelly beating at her face.

"I dare you to be angrier than me!" she screamed aloud to the storm. She let rain-tears roll down her face, her eyes and cheeks red from the power of the rain. Kinneret felt cold and numb all at once, yet she screamed out again toward the raging ocean, "I dare you! I dare you to be angrier than me! I dare you!"

"Hey, you! Get into the bus right now!" a teacher yelled at her. "What's the matter with you? We're facing a hurricane. Get in here!"

Kinneret raced to her bus. She jumped in and sat down in the first empty seat. Looking out the window into the darkness, she felt tired but somehow elated.

Chapter 5

Half an hour later, the bus pulled up to her driveway, and Kinneret got out. Her hood was still off as she ran to the front door soaking wet, and rang the doorbell.

Mr. Pfeiffer opened the door. "Kinneret, look at you, you're drenched," her father said as he led her into the kitchen and took her coat off.

Then, smiling, he cupped her cheeks in both of his large, warm hands and looked into his daughter's clear, beautiful eyes. He kissed her wet forehead and sat down. Kinneret sat across from him, feeling good. Safe.

"So tell me, how was school today? What did you learn?"

Kinneret looked into her father's face and wondered what she could tell him. She tried to recollect something wonderful she'd said or done, so her father would be proud. But her mind was filled with dozens of depressing phrases like:

"I don't like it when children lie to me."

"Kinneret doesn't know. She's so stupid."

"Go buy a brain, loser."

"Uh, you know what? Never mind."

"Is the circuit open or closed?"

"Who can say the aleph-bet backwards?"

"Can anyone help Kinneret?"

"A quarter is fifteen."

She wanted to tell him everything, but she couldn't.

"I helped someone in class today," she told her father, remembering how she had helped the woman who fixed the window.

"That's my girl."

"And we learned about circuit lightbulbs in science," she continued, not wanting to lose her father's attention.

"What did you learn about circuit lightbulbs?" her father asked.

"That when the bulb is open it's closed, and when the bulb is closed it's open," Kinneret proudly repeated. "And I think we have to bring a menorah for the principal tomorrow."

"The whole class?"

"Yes, everyone has to give him a present of a menorah tomorrow for Chanukah, so he can show the school how much we like him."

"I think maybe you misunderstood, Kinneret," her father said gently.

Kinneret looked down at her hands. "But that's what the teacher said," she insisted.

"Why don't you drink some hot chocolate while I finish studying with Micah," Mr. Pfeiffer suggested.

Kinneret was preparing the hot chocolate, when Meyer walked into the kitchen. "Hi, Meyer," Kinneret said, happy to see her brother.

"Hi," Meyer answered enthusiastically. "Guess what I know?"

"What?" Kinneret asked, warily.

"I know the whole times table."

"So? I do, too," Kinneret said defensively, hoping this wouldn't turn into a contest.

"Yeah, but you're in fourth grade. I bet in third grade you didn't know."

"Yes, I did!" Kinneret lied.

Meyer decided to change the subject. "You know what Uncle Alfred gave me today?" he began, in a teasing tone.

"What?" Kinneret asked.

"A quarter," Meyer said happily, displaying his quarter.

"That's not a quarter," Kinneret told him. "It's twenty-five cents!" She was happy that she knew about the change of rules before he did.

"A quarter and twenty-five cents is the same thing, silly," he said.

"Nope," Kinneret argued. "A quarter is fifteen cents. Maybe it used to be twenty-five cents, but now it's fifteen cents. Guaranteed."

Mrs. Pfeiffer walked into the kitchen. "What's all this arguing about?"

"Ima, right a quarter is twenty-five cents?" Meyer said.

"Yes."

"See?" Meyer told his sister.

Kinneret looked from her mother to her brother. "It's not fair," she shouted. "In school it was fifteen cents, and here it's twenty-five cents. How come we didn't change the rules here? It's not fair!" She ran to her room, slamming the door behind her.

Kinneret collapsed on her bed. "It's not fair," she said aloud to her ceiling. "They changed the rule back so quickly, how was I supposed to know? Every time I learn something, they change it. How does everyone else know?"

She got up and went into the bathroom. She walked up to the mirror and stared at her reflection.

"Do I look stupid?" she murmured. Kinneret saw that her eyes and nose and mouth were where they should be. Then she smoothed her eyebrows. She felt better once she concluded that she didn't look strange.

Kinneret placed both her hands on the mirror. "I think everything around me is like you," she told her reflection. "It's only a picture, a reflection. I can't really touch it or understand it. It changes and I don't even know it."

Kinneret went back to her bedroom and lay down on her bed.

She tried to summon the bird, to make her feel safe. She used every ounce of effort she could muster, but the bird wouldn't come. The bird never came at home, only in school.

She heard a knock at her door and knew it was her mother.

"Can I come in?" Mrs. Pfeiffer asked, and then walked in without waiting for a reply. She sat down on the edge of Kinneret's bed.

"Kinneret, what's the matter?"

Kinneret lay with her back to her mother. She didn't turn around because she knew that as soon as she looked into her mother's eyes and saw the pity that filled them, she would start to cry.

"There's something awfully wrong with me Ima," Kinneret whispered, feeling her voice about to crack.

"Kinneret, there's nothing wrong with you. You're wonderful," her mother said, desperately wanting to reassure this lonely child of hers. "Tell me why you're so upset." Mrs. Pfeiffer put her arm on her daughter's shoulder, but Kinneret shrugged it off.

She remained silent.

"I can't help you if you won't let me," Mrs. Pfeiffer said soothingly. "It's very hard to help people who don't want to be helped."

But I did call out for you, Kinneret thought accusingly. I called out a hundred times for you in school and you never came. Instead, you make me go back every day.

Mrs. Pfeiffer looked at this untouchable child of hers. She desperately wanted to pick her up and protect her from pain. At the same time, Kinneret longed to have her mother hold her tightly, yet her anger would not allow it.

"One day things'll seem better. You'll see, Kinneret," her mother told her.

Kinneret doubted that.

After her mother left the room, she walked over to her window and opened it. She looked out into the storm and stood unafraid as the lightning lit up the sky. The rain poured into her bedroom, and she heard the thunder, and saw the trees swaying in the turbulent wind. Then, facing the storm's rage, Kinneret began to cry. She cried hard, with real tears. The storm's wetness and her tears mingled on her face, forming an elixir of rage and pain.

Suddenly, she saw a bird, a white bird, a pigeon really, flapping its wings mightily, trying to find shelter from the storm.

She beckoned to it with her hands, still crying.

"Come here," she shouted, trying to coax the bird. "You're gonna die out there. The storm will kill you. Come in! Come in!" she yelled frantically.

But the bird could not hear her, or maybe it was too busy trying to survive. Kinneret watched as it flew out of sight, flapping its wings desperately.

She closed the window, still crying. She moved to her bed and lay down, dripping wet. She lay crying for a long time. She felt tired. So very tired.

Kinneret looked up at the ceiling.

God, she thought, her heart aching. I wish I could talk to everyone the way I talk to you, in thought, and not in words. It's so hard with words. They are always so mixed up. I know it's too much to ask to make everything easier, and I know it's too much to ask to make me smart, so I won't ask.

Just one thing I'll ask of you. When I dream tonight and they run after me, make me get to the safe place, God. Please!

Help me get there...

PART II

A teacher affects eternity;

he can never tell where his influence stops.

Henry Adams

Chapter 6

ONE YEAR LATER

"And last, but certainly not least, we have Kinneret," Mr. Jason, the assistant principal, told Miriam Klein. "A challenge you will no doubt live to regret," he added as he closed the file with a resolute thud.

Miriam was self-conscious about the half-smile she had on her face. Did she look like a typical, first-time, gung-ho, special education teacher — the kind she knew people like Mr. Jason resented? Or was she projecting her self-assured, calm, mature image? The kind of image her teachers had told her would open doors.

Cool it, Miriam coached herself. Stop analyzing everything. You've got the job already. Just relax.

Anyway, she *was* young and enthusiastic and self-assured. That's how she had gotten this plum of a job, one which even an experienced special-ed teacher would have loved. Only, the way Mr. Jason talked, it sounded like her plum of a job was really a rotten apple. He made the kids — especially this Kinneret girl — sound so...so...hopeless!

"Come on, Mrs. Klein," the assistant principal said, collecting the files and handing them over to her. "I'll show you where our new resource room is. If you need anything in the way of supplies, let me know. Your first student will be coming at 9:00 A.M., so you'd better acquaint yourself with those files in a hurry."

Miriam followed Mr. Jason to the resource room. Once inside, she felt more at ease. This was familiar ground. Without thinking, she wandered around the room, noticing how the light from the two windows gave the room a bright, cheerful look. She made a mental note to order construction paper and paste, which she saw was missing from the shelves. Then she remembered Mr. Jason.

She turned to thank him. But he was already gone.

Chapter 7

"No!" Kinneret shouted. "I won't go! You can't make me go!"

"Kinneret, don't be so angry. We're all trying to help you," her mother said, trying to defuse the explosive atmosphere in Kinneret's room.

"I don't need help. No one can help me anyway. Go help Meyer. Why doesn't Meyer have to go to the stupid sauce room?" Kinneret demanded, her voice rising.

"Kinneret!" Her father sliced the air with his voice and for a moment she thought he might hit her.

"It's called the resource room, Kinneret," her mother said gently.

"I don't care!" Kinneret declared, only more softly this time. "Why do I have to go?" she pleaded, close to tears.

"We've been through this already, Kinneret," her mother reminded her. "Remember all the tests you took with the learning specialist last summer? You need help. You can understand that, Kinneret. You're already in the fifth grade."

"I wish I wasn't."

"You're not the only one in school who has to go to the resource room. And you yourself said you don't understand what's going on in school."

"Next time I won't tell you anything," Kinneret threatened, with the knowledge of one who knows she has played all her cards and come up short.

She looked at her father and could see him making a physical effort to control his anger.

"Why does everyone think I'm so stupid?" Kinneret bawled, disgusted with herself because she could no longer hold back her tears. "Now everyone is going to know! Everyone! My teachers who already think I'm stupid, my friends, and Meyer, and everyone!"

Mrs. Pfeiffer tried to put an arm around her daughter, but Kinneret moved away.

"You're going to the resource room tomorrow, Kinneret," Mr. Pfeiffer insisted, "and that's that."

Kinneret knew she had no choice. It was always the same, no choices. She just wanted to save what face she could. "Please don't tell anyone," Kinneret implored, reaching out to her mother.

Her mother took her hand and kissed it. "Good night, Kinneret," she sighed. "You'll see. Things will work out."

"Only in storybooks," Kinneret replied, withdrawing her hand. "Never in real life." She saw a flash of pain cross her mother's brow, and she felt bad. But it's the truth, she told herself, as her parents left the room, closing the door behind them.

Kinneret felt hot, angry tears trickle down her cheeks and wind their way to her chin. With slumped shoulders, she looked through the wet blur that clouded her eyes toward the door and whispered defiantly, "You can't make me go. I'll run away."

Kinneret changed into pajamas, still crying. She knew her father would be in soon to put her sleeping baby sister into the crib across the room. She closed her eyes.

"I wish you would come now, bird. Come save me," she begged her magical friend.

But she knew it wouldn't appear. And besides, she wasn't afraid now, just angry. The bird only came when she was afraid.

"I wish you would come and take me away. We could go someplace safe, where everything makes sense and no one laughs or yells at you when you get all mixed up."

She heard her father gently push open her door. Kinneret closed her eyes and tried to breathe rhythmically. She heard him place her sleeping sister in the crib and mutter when he almost tripped over a sneaker that had been left in the middle of the floor of the darkened room. When he paused, she knew he was looking at her. She resisted the urge to turn around and see the expression on his face. In a matter of moments, he left.

"You know," she said into her pillow, "when I was littler, I was sure there had to be a safe place, somewhere. But now I don't believe there really is such a thing."

And it makes me sad, she finished in her heart.

Chapter 8

Kinneret was walking through a bright, grassy field. She was barefoot and wearing a long, white, cotton nightgown, the one she had
loved and worn often when she was in the third grade. Her lips were
formed into a soft smile, and she was holding a deep-red chrysanthe-
mum. Kinneret was gliding slowly through the field, her dark hair
billowing lightly over her face and shoulders.

Suddenly the field darkened. She saw metallic forms peeking at
her from behind big rocks, hundreds of them.

Soldiers.

Rifles and spears and swords surrounded her. She heard a shot
ring out. In slow motion, she turned to face the noise, but the noise
was everywhere now. The bullets were whizzing by her. The chry-
santhemum fell from her hand. She was alone against an army, and
for the first time, she could not run!

Kinneret faced the soldier closest to her and raised her arms in
surrender. But then another soldier rose from behind one of the
rocks. He was holding a spear the length of two men. She saw his

metal helmet glisten in the dying sun as he hunched forward and charged. Her face contorted as she screamed, only no sound came. His spear would tear her in half! He was close, so close. She could almost feel his breath upon her. Didn't he see that her arms were raised? Didn't he see she could not run?

NOOOOOOOO...

Chapter 9

Kinneret awoke with her head hanging off her bed. Her mouth was open and parched. Her pillow and blanket were on the floor, and she was sweating, soaking wet. Swallowing twice, she got up to look at her baby sister. Then she changed her pajamas. She looked at the digital clock near her bed: 4:27 A.M. Less than three hours left to sleep.

"Kinneret, good morning. It's SEVEN o'clock," she heard her mother say.

Kinneret opened her eyes reluctantly. "My head hurts, Ima," she said, feeling pain behind her eyes and around her temples.

"It'll pass."

"It really hurts. Why don't you ever believe me?" Kinneret whined.

"As soon as you're dressed, go to the kitchen and drink some juice."

"Juice never helps," Kinneret stated, feeling the pain spreading to the back of her head as well.

"Get dressed," Mrs. Pfeiffer commanded as she went to wake the baby.

Kinneret sat up slowly.

Forty minutes later, Kinneret sauntered into the kitchen. "Meyer, clear your plate. Ahuva, don't forget to pack your lunch. Kinneret, you're still not ready? The bus'll be here in five minutes. Go and brush your hair!"

"I won't go to the saucer room, Ima," Kinneret declared as she brushed her hair. She was using a shower brush because she couldn't remember where she had placed her own.

"Kinneret, we don't have time to discuss it now. Hurry up!" Mrs. Pfeiffer said emphatically.

Kinneret grabbed her coat and knapsack and ran out the front door.

"Have a good day," her mother called after her.

Kinneret made it to the bottom of the driveway just as the bus came. She got on, feeling her head begin to throb. Nausea hit her as she walked down the aisle. She sat down on the first empty bench she could find and concentrated on not throwing up. As the bus reached the bridge, her nausea passed and her school-ache began. It was a steady throbbing, bearable, just behind her eyes. Kinneret wished she could scream aloud — just scream. Then, she knew, she would feel better.

Mrs. Rubenstein entered the room calmly as the bell rang. The girls immediately found their places and started praying. Mrs. Rubenstein had been teaching the fifth grade for twenty-five years, and as far as she was concerned, she knew everything there was to know about ten-year-olds.

After prayers, at exactly nine o'clock, there was a knock on the door.

"Come in," Mrs. Rubenstein said, not getting up from her chair.

The door opened, and a smiling, hesitant young woman with brown mouse-colored hair entered the classroom. Instantly all eyes were upon her. The woman walked over to Mrs. Rubenstein's desk and spoke to her with her back to the class. Mrs. Rubenstein stood up and walked with the woman to the door, then faced her class.

"Girls, finish pages 17 and 18 in your workbooks," Mrs. Rubenstein said, standing half in, half out of the doorway. She wanted to make sure that the girls would know she was there.

Kinneret took out her Hebrew grammar workbook and opened it to page 17. She looked around her and saw that a few of the girls had started working. Others were excited about the sudden visitor. She saw Gila mouth to Melissa, "Who is that?" Melissa shrugged.

Mrs. Rubenstein stuck her head inside the classroom and said, "Kinneret, come out here for a minute, please."

Kinneret looked up, startled. Just her? No one else? This was definitely not good. She looked over at Dalia, seeking comfort. Dalia caught her eye and shrugged as if to say, "Sorry, what can I do?" Kinneret stood up, and her school-ache exploded somewhere deep inside her head.

The bird — she needed it badly. She summoned it, and it came. She wanted it to take her on its back and fly far, far away. Only it wouldn't. It flew beside her, big and comforting. Her hand rested on its enormous back as she made the long trek from her seat to the door, very aware of twenty-four pairs of eyes on her back. Kinneret walked out to the hall, where Mrs. Rubenstein was talking with the strange woman.

Miriam watched as the child solemnly approached and noticed Kinneret's dark hair and fine, yet by no means beautiful, features. Her eyes were the most striking thing about her, deep-set and light gray. They had the ability to look into a person, and also to look through them. They were penetrating. Breathtaking.

"Kinneret, is there something wrong with your arm?" Mrs. Rubenstein asked, concerned. Kinneret looked up dumbly, vaguely aware that she had been addressed, but unable to concentrate simultaneously on the bird and the teacher.

"Kinneret, I asked you if there was something wrong with your arm!" Mrs. Rubenstein repeated more firmly. Kinneret looked at her arm, which was on the bird's back.

"No," she answered, drawing her arm closer to her body. She felt the bird slipping away from her. Disoriented, she looked down at her side.

"This is Mrs. Klein. She will be your resource room teacher."

"Call me Miriam," Mrs. Klein said enthusiastically. She wanted to comfort the ill-at-ease child in front of her. She put her hand on Kinneret's shoulder, inadvertently brushing the bird's feathers. Kinneret instinctively stepped back. But it was too late — the bird vanished.

Kinneret closed her eyes tightly for a moment, but when she realized the bird would not return she opened them. She trembled slightly as she realized she was standing in front of two teachers who were talking about her. And she was alone.

Miriam saw Kinneret shiver and wondered if the child was sick.

"Kinneret, go into the classroom and bring me your Torah test, please," Mrs. Rubenstein commanded.

Kinneret opened the door to the classroom. Again all eyes looked up as she entered the classroom. She stared at the floor on her way back to her seat. She fished out the test paper from her knapsack. It was crumpled and slightly ripped. She tried to straighten it out. Kinneret didn't have to look at the paper to remember her grade. The thirty-four was burned into her memory.

Kinneret left the room again. She knew that the bird would not appear. Like her, it didn't want to be noticed. Like her, it wanted to stay invisible. Unlike her, it had a choice.

"Kinneret, what did I write on your test?" Mrs. Rubenstein asked, when she reached the two teachers.

Kinneret looked at her test paper. The teacher had written all sorts of things on the test, she thought. What does she want me to tell her?

"This is not what I asked for," Kinneret read out in a barely audible whisper. She felt humiliated. When Mrs. Rubenstein didn't tell her to stop reading, she looked for other remarks. "You didn't answer the question," she read, scanning for yet other remarks, some of which she could hardly read.

"I meant, read what I wrote next to your grade," Mrs. Rubenstein snapped, visibly upset.

Kinneret, finally realizing what the teacher wanted, read clearly, "See me."

"Kinneret, you must learn responsibility," she suddenly scolded. "I cannot run after you. You did not see me as I asked."

Kinneret raised her head. "I did. I did see you," she said, indignantly.

Kinneret didn't understand. Why had the teacher written on the top of the test that Kinneret should look at her? Kinneret saw her every day. Did she have to wait until the teacher saw her seeing her?

The teacher chose to ignore Kinneret's remarks, rather than call her a liar. But she was not happy with the way her student was behaving. "Kinneret, you must stop contradicting," she scolded. "You must apply yourself more. Lazy children never learn much."

Miriam, feeling uneasy and annoyed, cut in. "Perhaps Kinneret and I should get to the resource room now, before the period is up."

"All right, then," Mrs. Rubenstein agreed, looking at the time. It was almost nine-thirty, and she still had an entire lesson to teach.

She had more to say, but Miriam quickly turned to Kinneret and said, "Come on, we don't have much time left," leaving Mrs. Rubenstein without anyone to complain to.

Kinneret walked down the hall, arm's length from Miriam. She was ashamed that Miriam had witnessed her teacher's lashing criticism. Her head was steadily throbbing.

"Kinneret, your parents spoke to you about the resource room, didn't they?" Miriam smiled warmly, hoping to break the ice.

Kinneret nodded. She distrusted smiley adults. Long experience had taught her that they only smiled at you as long as they thought you were smart. As soon as they saw you didn't understand, they stopped smiling.

They turned left at the corner and then made another right. Then they walked down two flights of stairs.

"Do you have any brothers and sisters?" Miriam asked, persistently.

Kinneret nodded again.

"How many?"

Kinneret hesitated, then asked, "Including me?"

"Okay," Miriam said, realizing Kinneret had taken her question very literally. "Yes, including you."

"I have four sisters with me, and two brothers," Kinneret said, feeling uneasy.

"So you're one of four sisters."

"Yes." Kinneret breathed deeply, relieved that she had answered properly. That question was always so confusing; sometimes they wanted to know with you included and sometimes without.

"This is the resource room," Miriam announced. They stopped in front of the out-of-the-way room on the ground floor. "Just pull the doorknob and we're in," she said pleasantly, taking a step back.

Kinneret swallowed. "Which way?" she asked.

"What?" Miriam asked, puzzled. Then, recovering quickly and re-alizing that Kinneret didn't know the difference between push and pull, she said, "Toward you, to you."

Kinneret slowly pulled the door open and stepped in.

Colors, lots of colors, greeted Kinneret as she stepped into the room. It was bright and neat, and there was a chestful of drawers, with names and flowers on each drawer. The walls were decorated with pictures of balloons, and on the balloons were words. Big words, colored and pleasant to read. At the far end of the room, near the windows, Kinneret could see an empty wall with yellow paper stuck on it.

"That's where we hang up the children's work," Miriam said, no-ticing Kinneret looking at the sun-lit wall.

I'm NEVER going to hang up anything of mine there, Kinneret thought.

"Come, Kinneret, let's sit down. Oh, wait, I want to show you your drawer." Miriam walked over to the third drawer from the top. "See, this is your drawer. It has your name on it."

Kinneret looked at the drawer, at her name, and at the yellow sunflower next to it. It was beautiful. Her eyes showed her pleasure, even though her lips would not.

"You can decorate this drawer however you want. It's yours."

"Can I cover my name?" Kinneret whispered at once.

"If you'd like," Miriam responded, realizing for the first time the depth of Kinneret's low self-image. "We can do that at the end of the lesson. But first, I want to know if you understand why you're here." Miriam took a seat and motioned for Kinneret to take the one oppo-site her.

Kinneret sat down, her pulse quickening, as she realized now would come the questions. Questions that would show how stupid she was.

"Because I don't learn good," Kinneret whispered, angry at herself and at this woman whom she was certain would harp on her weak points and lay them out on the table for inspection.

"Kinneret," Miriam said, with as much enthusiasm as she could muster, "I believe that you can learn great!"

You don't know me, Kinneret thought, and waited for the period to end.

Chapter 10

"Kinneret, how was it?" Mrs. Pfeiffer asked, hugging her daughter as she opened the front door.

"How was what?" Kinneret asked in return, taking off her knapsack. She breathed deeply, and the smell of meatballs made her mouth water. She realized how hungry she was.

"Mrs. Klein. The resource room," her mother explained.

"Oh," Kinneret replied. It seemed like so much had happened since that morning at the resource room.

It had been downhill after Mrs. Klein, and she had gotten into another fight with Gila.

"I don't want to go again," Kinneret said, although with less conviction than the night before.

Kinneret's mother put her hand on her daughter's cheek. "I can see you didn't have a good day today," she said softly.

Kinneret sighed. "No, I never have a good day at school."

"Well, you'll have a good day at home then. I made your favorite supper."

Kinneret smiled for the first time that day.

"E-et, E-et," Miri, the baby called out when she saw Kinneret.

Kinneret held her arms out, and Miri ran into them. "I missed you today, Miri," Kinneret crooned to her almost-two-year-old sister, kissing her on the top of her soft hair.

"She called for you all day," Mrs. Pfeiffer said. "Watch her, please, until I finish making supper, and put your knapsack and coat in your room." Kinneret set her sister down on the floor beside her and carried her knapsack into her room, with Miri close behind.

Kinneret heard the doorbell ring and knew it was her older sister, Ahuva.

"Kinneret, get the door please," her mother shouted.

"Coming," Kinneret yelled, scooping up her sister. She opened the door.

"Boy, am I hungry," Ahuva said, walking in. "Hello, Miri," she cooed, stretching out her hands.

Miri laid her head on Kinneret's neck. "Me want E-et," she insisted, clutching Kinneret tightly.

"Me want food," Ahuva replied off-hand, trying not to show that she felt rejected.

"Kinneret, come look! I won some new marbles for our collection," Kinneret heard Meyer call out.

She ran into Meyer's room with Miri still on her hip, and found Meyer and Micah sitting around a very large pile of marbles. Micah kept trying to put the marbles on the top of the pile. He was getting frustrated at the landslides this caused.

"I won seven blue ones. Look," Meyer said, as he handed a blue marble to Kinneret.

Kinneret looked fleetingly at Meyer, feeling inadequate because she hadn't won a single marble to add to their collection. She was a poor player, so she had only played a few times. She stood out as the only shooter to lose all her marbles because she never managed to hit another one. The way she added to the collection was by asking for marbles when they got presents.

Kinneret raised the blue marble to the light, eyeing it from different angles. There was something dazzling about marbles.

"It's beautiful," she declared. Meyer beamed.

"Can I be in your collection, too?" Micah whined.

"We'll think about it. Maybe when you're our age," Meyer said.

"Well, we're not the same age," Kinneret informed him. "I'm a year and two months older than you!"

"So what?"

"So, we're not the same age," Kinneret repeated. She looked at the pile of marbles, thinking of something to say that would change the subject.

"Me want dis arble," Miri announced.

"Smart girl, you want the blue marble. Blue is the best!" Meyer chanted.

"Bue da best!" Miri repeated.

"You are the smartest. Just the smartest!" Meyer whooped.

"Smatet!" Miri echoed, laughing. She liked the sound of the word and repeated, "Smatet!"

The boys laughed.

"No!" Kinneret whispered fiercely to her little sister, hugging her tightly. Miri stopped talking, not knowing what she had done wrong.

"Don't say that. You don't have to be smartest. I love you even if you're not the smartest."

The baby pushed Kinneret away and started to cry.

Chapter 11

"How was the first day at school?" Yehudah Klein asked his wife, Miriam, as they sat down for supper.

"Strange, pathetic. The whole thing just doesn't make sense. The kids start school in September. We special-ed teachers don't get to start with them until now, mid-November. The principal insists that for the first year of the program, we only work with the first through third-grades and get the near-hopeless kids from older grades. The rest of the kids are left to flounder. Meanwhile, it gets harder and harder on them. Next year they'll be in worse shape than they are now."

"Meanwhile, do what you can with the kids you have," Yehudah suggested, passing his wife the salad. He hoped that Miriam would forget about this topic. He had heard little else for the past two months.

"But it's more than that," Miriam blazed, ignoring the salad bowl that hovered over the table in Yehudah's outstretched hand. "I worked with seven kids today, six of whom were in the first through third-grades. Three of them could barely read at all. One second-grader asked me what the story was about before she read it. I told her it was about a dwarf. She puts her finger on the page and tells me not to read with her, so I watch her. Do you know what she did?"

"No," Yehudah sighed, putting down the salad bowl. "Tell me what she did."

"She followed along with her finger and told me the story of Snow White and the seven dwarfs. She flipped the pages while she was doing this."

"So?" Yehudah naively wondered.

"The story was *not* about Snow White!"

"Do you want some chicken?" Yehudah ventured.

"One kid could barely write at all," Miriam continued. "I couldn't read a single word he wrote." She looked over at her husband. "I'm sorry," she said sympathetically. "Are you hungry?"

"How did you guess?" he asked.

She broke out into a smile. "Then we'll eat now, and I won't say a word more about my students."

"Can I have that in writing?" Yehudah asked, the beginnings of a smile on his lips.

Miriam wagged a finger at her husband. "Don't be facetious," she said, laughing in spite of herself. "Now, tell me about your day."

"Architecture school isn't anywhere as interesting as life in the special education fast lane," Yehudah said with a twinkle in his eye. "If we have any problematic circles or squares, I'll let you know."

Miriam crumpled her napkin, and with the accuracy of a former high school basketball champ, she threw it at Yehudah's forehead. It bounced off his head into his salad.

"Hey, not fair," he protested feebly, crumpling his own napkin into a ball.

"Who said life was fair!" Miriam exclaimed, snatching the napkin out of his hand.

"You special-ed teachers are a tough breed," Yehudah chuckled as he bit into his chicken.

An hour later, they were in the kitchen, washing and drying the dishes.

"You know what really irked me about today?" Miriam asked, turning toward her husband, her hands full of suds.

"Let me guess. One of your students?" Yehudah replied with a grin.

"This one girl I worked with, a ten-year-old," Miriam continued, ignoring her husband's sarcasm. "She only whispered when I spoke to her and looked so uncomfortable. She didn't smile, and I told her about every joke I know. I did everything but dance on the table. But I couldn't reach her."

"Some people just need a while to warm up to others," Yehudah suggested seriously.

"Yeah, maybe," Miriam replied, unconvinced.

"Or maybe, like some other people I know, she just didn't think your jokes were funny," Yehudah continued, hiding his face under a towel.

"Stop being a baby," Miriam said.

"Are you holding any napkins in your hand?" When he didn't get an answer, Yehudah peeked above the towel.

Miriam continued washing the dishes. "Her teacher was so mean," she angrily explained. "Innocently mean, but still so...so...damaging. This child has a real language problem. She didn't know the difference between push and pull. When I asked her how many hours were in a day, she asked me if I meant in the summer or in the winter, because in the summer there are more hours in a day."

"Hey, that's not so strange. It sort of makes weird sense," Yehudah said, feeling his wife might be reading too much into the girl's words.

"You think it's normal for a ten-year-old girl to be unable to tell me that there are twenty-four hours in a day and seven days in a week? She was able to recite all the days of the week, in order. But when I asked her how many days there are in a week she said, 'Including today?' You think it makes sense for a girl her age not to be able to tell me if there are six, seven, or eight days from Monday to Monday? For her to want to know if I was counting both Mondays, or none, or one?"

Miriam shut the faucet, leaving both her hands on it. She looked into the sink, watching the last of the bubbles swirling around as they floated down the drain.

"She didn't want her name on her drawer. She was ashamed and made me cover it up. The world must be such a confusing place for her."

"Hey, it's confusing for us all."

"But we, at least, have a fair shot."

"Who said the world was fair?" Yehudah reminded her.

"You're right. But I still don't understand how she has been sitting in a classroom for five years without anyone saying boo.

"And what's my part in all this? I get a child who's had only negative experiences for five straight years. She gets thrown into my lap for a short time each day. Then she's thrown back again into her classroom, where no one understands, or even tries to understand her, for the rest of the day. Talk about fighting the tide!"

"You'll do fine," Yehudah assured her, taking his wife's hand in his own. "It's what you've always wanted to do. And not all the teachers are ignorant."

"It's just that she's already in fifth grade. She's clearly got a learning disability. Where has everyone been?"

Yehudah looked at his wife. "Have you considered that maybe some teachers don't know what a learning disability is?"

"Please! How can you be a teacher these days and not know what a learning disability is?"

"There are probably plenty of teachers in the system who have been there since the year one. But look on the bright side. Now you have the younger kids, and you *can* help them," Yehudah said, hoping to end the discussion.

"But you don't understand," Miriam protested. "So many kids from the older classes need help. Every class must have at least one or two. There are laws to make kids go to school, but no laws to protect kids who get hurt in the process. And kids soon pick up on their teacher's indifference. Before long they stop trying and turn themselves off, not just for a few days — but for years. It becomes a way of life. They even begin to call themselves 'stupid' and it becomes a self-fulfilling prophecy. It's the system, Yehudah. It's this archaic system."

"I see you're on the warpath, Miriam," Yehudah said, half taunting, half serious. "But, if you ask me, I think you're being naive."

"Why, because I think the system stinks?"

"No," Yehudah replied easily, "because with all that, you still think you can change it."

Chapter 12

"Kinneret, don't forget, you have to leave class at nine o'clock sharp."

"Sh, Ima!" Kinneret said, putting her finger to her lips. "Everyone will hear." She looked around the busy kitchen.

"Everyone is eating breakfast. They're all in a hurry. No one is listening," her mother assured her.

"Ima, I don't want to go. When I come back to class, everyone asks where I went."

"What do you answer?"

"That it's none of their business."

"Kinneret, you can tell them. You have nothing to be ashamed of."

"Then how come no one else goes?" Kinneret asked, her voice starting to break.

"We're not going through that again, not now. Come on, hurry up! Your bus will be here in five minutes."

"My head hurts real bad, Ima, and I'm nauseous," Kinneret whimpered, trying to play on her mother's sympathies one last time. "Can I stay home with you? Just today?"

Mrs. Pfeiffer looked into her daughter's gray eyes. There was pain there, and fear. For a second she wavered. Perhaps leaving in the middle of class was too embarrassing; perhaps going to a regular school was just too difficult for her.

Mr. Pfeiffer had been watching the discussion between his wife and daughter from the kitchen entrance and realized that his wife was about to give in.

"Everyone goes to school today!" he announced, striding into the kitchen. "I don't want anyone without temperature staying home."

Kinneret knew it was hopeless now.

Her mother quickly recovered her resolve and said, "Kinneret, hurry up or you'll miss the bus."

Kinneret emitted an involuntary whimper as she grabbed her coat and her knapsack and ran out the door. She sprinted down the driveway, the cold air whipping her face. Shivering, Kinneret jumped on the bus. She put her coat on and sat down, feeling weak.

Before she knew it, Kinneret fell asleep and only awoke when the bus had come to a full stop in front of the school. She felt cheated because she had not been able to mentally prepare herself for the day.

When the class finished prayers, it was five to nine. Her new digital watch saved her the embarrassment of asking someone for the time. She was sure that whomever she asked would want to know why she needed to know the time.

"Girls, Torah time! Who remembers from our last class what makes an animal kosher?"

Kinneret looked up, her eyes shining because she knew, yes, she definitely knew the answer. It has a hole along the whole of its foot and it eats food and swallows and eats it again. But how do you say it without everyone laughing at you?

I forgot the words to say it in short, Kinneret thought helplessly. I know it. I just can't remember it when she asks.

Frustrated, Kinneret gazed out toward the ocean. It was high tide, and the waters appeared greenish blue. She looked out over the calm waves, beyond the squawking seagulls. The ocean was gigantic and strong, and comforting, yet it never asked for anything in return. It only gave of its beauty. Kinneret squinted, trying to block out everything around her but the ocean.

"Kinneret!" a sharp voice sounded, piercing her thoughts.

Startled, Kinneret looked forward, a chill running down her spine. The school-ache erupted like a volcano. She felt rivulets of pain sizzling her brain. Kinneret wished — needed — to disappear.

"You're not on the right page," Mrs. Rubenstein scolded.

Kinneret flipped some pages, not sure where the right page was. The teacher gave her a penetrating look and went on with the lesson.

Then Kinneret called the bird. She summoned it hard, and it did not disappoint her. Almost at once, she felt herself astride the bird, over the ocean, flying high. It was beautiful, sparkling, pain-free. She could feel the urgency of its strong wings as it led her far, far away from the classroom.

"Beep-beep." She heard her watch beep the hour.

Nine o'clock! Oh NO!

She looked at the teacher, hoping for some sign that would indicate she could leave. She had told Miriam she would come by herself because she did not want the girls to see Miriam waiting at the door.

But how could she leave?

9:01.

How would she ask if she could leave? And how could she do it without everyone watching?

"Who can tell me what the signs of a kosher fish are?"

Many hands shot up.

"Yes, Dalia?"

"The fish has to have fins and scales."

"Very good. That is correct."

9:04.

Kinneret began to sweat.

I'll raise my hand, she thought to herself, I'll raise my hand on the count of three. One, two, three —

I can't. WHAT SHOULD I DO? What will I say when she calls on me? What if she doesn't call on me for a really long time?

9:07.

The school-ache was starting again, pounding behind her eyes. Pain.

Why isn't she telling me to go? Has she forgotten? Maybe she isn't saying anything on purpose, because she hates me, and she wants Miriam to hate me, too.

9:09.

There was a terrible ache, throbbing, steadily throbbing at the base of her skull.

9:10.

RAISE YOUR HAND!

Kinneret lifted her hand hesitantly, as high as her chin. She hunched her shoulders forward.

"What is it?" Mrs. Rubenstein asked, slightly annoyed.

"It's nine o'clock. I have to go," she mumbled.

"I can't hear you," Mrs. Rubenstein said, walking over to Kinneret's desk.

Kinneret pointed to her watch.

"Oh my, it's 9:10 already. You were supposed to leave at nine o'clock. Why didn't you go? Tomorrow at exactly nine o'clock I want you to get up quietly and leave. Do you understand that?"

Kinneret understood, and she was certain that the rest of the class understood as well. Red-faced, she stood up and made her way to the front of the classroom and then to the door.

Now I'm late, she thought to herself, and everyone is going to say that I'm not responsible.

She walked quickly down the hall, afraid to run and break the rules. She turned right and then went down the staircase.

It must be here somewhere, she thought. Do I turn right or left?

Kinneret didn't know, so she continued walking.

"'It has to be here. Please let it be here," she whispered frantically.

The hallway was deserted. Kinneret continued walking and turned left again at the corner. Kinneret's sense of direction was poor under the best of conditions. Under pressure she didn't stand a chance.

The librarian was coming down the hall. She would ask her. But if she asked the librarian for the resource room, the librarian would KNOW where Kinneret was going.

Kinneret watched as the librarian passed, wishing she would say something to her.

It was all so confusing.

Kinneret walked faster, half running, feeling the sameness of each door, each corridor, confused, desperate. Everything looked the same!

And then it happened.

Her school-ache exploded into a million pieces!

Kinneret grabbed the wall, shutting her eyes tightly, grimacing and clenching her teeth so she would not cry. She fell to the floor, her eyes still shut.

Everyone will be so angry at me, she thought, as she gave into the pain, letting it take its course.

"I need you now, bird. I need you real bad, real, real bad. Please come," she begged.

And the bird came. It picked Kinneret up and let her leave all her pain and frustration behind. It took her out, over the ocean. She was so happy. The bird was soft and accepting, and so strong.

Chapter 13

It was nearing nine-thirty. Miriam had already peeked into Kinneret's classroom. She saw Kinneret was not there and wondered if perhaps Kinneret had run away.

Miriam walked through the wide hallways of the school. What a big school this is, she thought.

On the second floor of the school, she spotted Kinneret's dark hair from afar. Approaching, she called out softly, "Kinneret."

Kinneret did not respond. She just stood in the hallway, a blank look on her face.

"Kinneret," Miriam said again, only much louder. "Kinneret," she called a third time, touching Kinneret's shoulder, turning her around, and suddenly noticing the impassive expression on her face.

Startled, Kinneret stepped back. In an instant, the bird was gone.

Miriam smiled. "I didn't mean to scare you."

Kinneret stared at her teacher and then looked down at the floor.

"Let's go to the resource room. We only have fifteen minutes left."

Miriam started to walk down the hall. Kinneret walked silently alongside her. Miriam tried to think of something to say. Should she ask Kinneret why she was late? Maybe she should just leave it alone and make sure to come for her tomorrow.

Meanwhile, Kinneret wondered why Miriam hadn't said anything about her lateness.

"We're here," Miriam announced, as they reached the door of the resource room. "Just pull the doorknob, and we're in."

Kinneret hesitated, then remembered that to open the door, she had to pull the doorknob toward her. She pulled it and entered, eyeing the drawers by the closet. She was relieved that her name was still covered.

Miriam took out a bag filled with candies.

"Pick any one you want, Kinneret."

"No thank you," Kinneret replied softly. She had been bribed before to learn, but when she tried and failed, she always felt guilty about taking the candies. No. No bribes this time.

They had been talking only a short time when the school bell rang. "I guess it's time to walk you back to class," Miriam said.

"No," Kinneret replied quickly, "I can walk by myself."

Miriam looked at Kinneret. "Are you sure?"

Kinneret nodded. "When I go out, I make a right and go up the stairs?" she asked, furrowing her brows and feeling uncomfortable.

Miriam could see that Kinneret didn't really know the way. But she didn't want her to lose her dignity.

"How about if I walk you to the hall of your classroom and you walk the rest of the way by yourself?" she suggested.

Gratefully, Kinneret agreed.

Miriam led the way.

"This is such a big school. It's so easy to get lost," she remarked.

Kinneret looked up at Miriam and nodded. Did Miriam really understand?

They walked up the two flights of stairs. When Kinneret's classroom came into view, Miriam said, "I'll wait for you here tomorrow morning at nine o'clock. Is that all right?"

Kinneret nodded, relieved. Now she was sure. Miriam understood.

Kinneret quietly entered the classroom just as Mrs. Rubenstein asked the girls to take out their grammar books. Kinneret felt several pairs of eyes following her across the room.

"I want everyone to open to page 12. Rows 1 and 2, do examples 1 through 6. Rows 3 and 4, do examples 7 to 12. Row 5, do examples 13 through 18. We will go over the answers out loud together before recess."

Kinneret sat down and took out her book, feeling small and bewildered. What am I supposed to do? she wondered.

Mrs. Rubenstein sat down at her desk and started marking some papers.

The class began to work. Kinneret looked around, wide-eyed. If only someone would tell her what she was expected to do. She leaned over to her right and whispered to Dalia, "Dalia, what does row 5 have to do?"

Dalia glanced over to the teacher and, seeing it was safe to reply, answered hurriedly, "Thirteen to eighteen."

Kinneret opened to page 13. There was so much to do!

How will I do through page 18 until recess? It's too many pages.

She looked at the page: "Fill in the appropriate word," it said.

Because Kinneret was used to being given tasks which were impossible for her to fulfill, she didn't hesitate. She figured that if that was what the teacher said, the other kids were probably able to do it.

By the time the teacher told the class to stop working, Kinneret had done only three examples, all of them wrong.

"All right, class," Mrs. Rubenstein announced at a quarter to eleven. "We'll start from Cynthia, and everyone in her turn, will read out one exercise."

Cynthia began reading, and before long Kinneret realized she was on the wrong page. She frantically started turning pages, but it was hopeless. Resigned to failure, she stared out toward the ocean, seeking comfort, but there was too much noise, too much tension in the air for her to concentrate enough to call the bird.

Dalia was looking at her, mouthing something. What was it?

Oh, it was page 12. Then why did she tell me page 13?

Miraculously, Kinneret found the proper exercise. "*Kova,*" Dalia managed to whisper, before she read aloud exercise 14.

Kova? What am I supposed to do with that, Kinneret wondered.

But before she could think further, Mrs. Rubenstein said, "Kinneret, it's your turn. Which word did you fill in?"

Kinneret looked helplessly over at Dalia. Dalia stared at her, nodding.

"Kova," Kinneret gulped.

Mrs. Rubenstein nodded and called on Ahuva.

Kinneret breathed hard, wondering what she had said and why it was right.

"Thank you," she gratefully mouthed to Dalia, after she had calmed down. Dalia smiled in return.

"Girls, after I return your Joshua tests you may go out for recess. Dalia, Melissa, Sharon, Gila, Cynthia, Arielle, Kinneret, Sara..."

Each girl went up in turn to receive her test. Kinneret, amid the whoops and cheers of the girls who already received their tests, approached the teacher's desk. She looked at her teacher hesitantly.

Mrs. Rubenstein placed the test hastily in Kinneret's hand, glancing up briefly.

I failed again, Kinneret thought without even looking at the grade, fluent in the unspoken sign language of teachers.

"How did you do?" she heard Dalia ask her.

"I didn't look at my test yet."

"So what are you waiting for?"

Kinneret opened her test paper and looked at her grade.

Twenty-two percent! Ashamed, she knew she had to say something to Dalia, but what? The words "Oh, how annoying, I only got an eighty again. How about you?" just tripped out of her mouth. What choice did she have?

"I got a ninety."

"Good for you," Kinneret replied cheerfully, stuffing her test paper into her knapsack.

"Are you coming to recess?"

"Yeah, in a minute."

Dalia left. Kinneret kept her head in her knapsack, stubbornly refusing to let tears leave her eyes.

"I really got a twenty-two," she wanted to tell Dalia, but she knew she wouldn't. She had lied to Dalia a thousand times and hated herself for it, and a thousand times she had been afraid that Dalia would ask to see the test. And sometimes it was hard to remember what marks she had told to whom.

She clenched her fists tightly. She felt a school-ache coming on. It was like her rage, just under the surface, always very near to exploding.

Chapter 14

"I hope we don't play dodge ball today," Kinneret said to Dalia as they were changing into pants for gym class.

"Why? I thought you liked ball games."

"Well, I don't," Kinneret answered darkly. "They're too competing."

"What?" asked Dalia. "Oh, you mean competitive," she corrected.

"That's what I said," Kinneret replied defensively.

"If I were you, I wouldn't care. You can cream almost anyone."

"No I can't," Kinneret sighed. "I usually miss. It's just that when I hit someone with the ball, it hurts."

"I wouldn't mind being able to do that. You're lucky you're so strong."

"It's not strongness, it's anger," Kinneret tried to explain. "I wish there didn't always have to be winners and losers."

"You guys had better run into the gym or you'll be late," Melissa screamed out.

"Thanks, Melissa, we're coming," Dalia yelled back, as she and

Kinneret made their way to the gym.

"All right, girls, I hope you're in a running mood. I want everyone to run ten laps around the gym."

The class groaned.

"Come on girls, we want to work those muscles."

Kinneret started to run. She was on her turf now. She loved the sensation of running, feeling warm wind on her face, hearing the soft pounding of her sneakers on the wooden gym floor. She wouldn't begin to sweat until after the fifth lap, and she always ended up running extra laps until the other girls had finished.

Mrs. Carmel, the gym teacher, blew her whistle. The girls stopped running and collapsed on the floor.

"Good, girls. You ran well. Now take a one-minute break."

Kinneret caught Dalia's eye, and smiled.

"Form a line," Mrs. Carmel ordered, after their minute was up. "We'll begin vaulting."

The girls dutifully formed a line and Sara self-consciously raised her hand.

"Yes, Sara?" Mrs. Carmel asked with a smile.

"Can I please sit on the side? Vaulting is scary, and I'm no good at it," Sara said, on the verge of tears.

Mrs. Carmel took pity on the heavy, uncoordinated child in front of her. "Don't worry, Sara," she assured her, "you don't have to succeed, just try. I give good grades to kids who show me that they are working hard, trying, and doing their best. That's the most important thing. Even if someone can't get over the horse, if I see that she's trying and doing her best, she'll get at least an eighty."

Sara smiled.

"Why?" Kinneret heard herself ask aloud, her clear gray eyes questioning.

"Kinneret, I'm surprised at you," Mrs. Carmel admonished. "You're more sensitive than that. We don't all have the same ability to run and jump. Everyone has to utilize what they have, to the best of their ability."

Mrs. Carmel went to set up the horse.

But why? Kinneret asked again, soundlessly. Why is it that in gym no one cares whether you're good or not? She gets smiled at, whether she's good or not. She gets a good mark even if she can't do it. In all the other classes, no one cares if you try or not; if you don't do well, they fail you. Period. Why is it different here?

Is it because in gym the teacher can SEE you trying? That's not fair! I'm trying as hard as I can even if the teacher can't see. Why doesn't it count? Sara can't vault the horse, and I can't understand Torah, English and math. So what? So what if my brain can't run or leap or vault? So what if my brain just walks very, very slowly? Why isn't that okay, too?

"All right, girls," Mrs. Carmel announced after all the girls had lined up in front of the horse. "Begin with straddle jumps. Don't worry, I'm right here guarding you."

Miranda took off and landed with a thud, straddle-legged on the horse.

"I see that you're trying, Miranda. But you have to maintain a ninety-degree angle over the horse so you land on the other side. Remember, only your hands can touch the vault."

Miranda nodded.

"Good. That's right, Cynthia. Push more with your hands," Mrs. Carmel said, encouraging the second girl. The next few girls straddled the horse but lost their balance on the way down.

Finally, it was Kinneret's turn. She took a deep breath and concentrated. She ran, jumped, placed her hands on top of the horse, and pushed off, landing perfectly in a standing position.

"Kinneret, that was beautiful," Mrs. Carmel declared. A few of the girls on line even clapped.

Kinneret nodded, feeling proud.

"One of her legs was bent," Gila called out from the line.

"Straighten both legs next turn," Mrs. Carmel said absently to Kinneret. "Dalia, it's your turn."

Kinneret walked to the end of the line, staring at Gila through narrowed eyes.

Gila smiled back sweetly.

"Don't think about her," Dalia advised, having just completed her jump and joining the back of the line. "She's just jealous because your vault was good."

On Kinneret's next vault, she took the jump off the wrong foot and couldn't right herself. She landed with her stomach on the horse. Red-faced, Kinneret looked up at her teacher.

"I got mixed up," she whispered.

"Don't worry. You'll get it next turn."

If only she were consistent, Mrs. Carmel thought. She can do something beautifully one time, and the next time fall on her face for no apparent reason. I wonder why that is?

Kinneret's next vault was strong, her timing exact. She pushed the horse lightly with her hands, straddled her legs, and landed with her feet together on the floor mats.

"Good job."

Kinneret returned to the back of the line.

"All right, girls," Mrs. Carmel said twenty minutes later, "let's play dodge ball."

Mrs. Carmel divided up the girls. Kinneret noticed that Dalia was on the other team, but unfortunately, Gila was on hers.

Mrs. Carmel blew her whistle. "PLAY BALL!"

The other team had the ball. Tzila threw it to her captain.

The captain threw the ball back, over the girls' heads. Kinneret stayed in the back, using her speed to avoid the ball, hoping to stay inconspicuous so no one would get her out.

The ball was intercepted by Kinneret's team and passed to their captain, Ilana, who passed the ball to Kinneret. Kinneret caught the ball, saw Dalia turning to run — less then a foot away from her — but threw the ball back to Ilana.

"Hey, not fair! You could have gotten Dalia out!" Gila yelled. "Why didn't you?"

I can't hit Dalia, Kinneret thought. I could never hit Dalia.

"She ran away too fast," Kinneret replied tartly. "Anyway, I don't have to answer to you."

"Girls, no fighting on the court," Mrs. Carmel commanded.

"You're such an idiot, Kinneret," Gila whispered.

Kinneret stood still for a moment, waiting for the wave of anger to pass, then replied, "I'd rather be an idiot than be anything like you." But Gila was already out of earshot.

Soon there were five girls out on each team. Kinneret felt her adrenalin pumping.

I can't get out, she thought desperately. I have to win, I have to win. If you get out, you don't count.

She intercepted the ball from the other team, held it in the crook of her right arm, and as the rage inside her reached a crescendo, hurled it at Nina. The speeding ball veered toward Arielle, who held out her arms. Kinneret watched as the ball flew into Arielle's outstretched arms, slammed into her stomach, and bounced to the floor. Arielle doubled over and started to cry. Mrs. Carmel called, "Time out!"

Kinneret dashed over to Arielle. "I'm sorry, Arielle," she said, feeling miserable. "Are you okay?"

"Kinneret, you must throw the ball more gently," Mrs. Carmel cautioned. "Is that clear?"

"I can't help it," Kinneret stubbornly insisted. She was embarrassed and angry that everyone blamed her for everything that she couldn't help.

"Yes, you can," Mrs. Carmel shot back.

Kinneret opened her mouth to try and explain what happened to her when she held the ball, that something scary from inside her took control. But she could not find the words.

"Can I sit on the side and keep Arielle company?" she pleaded.

"No!" Mrs. Carmel stated emphatically.

Kinneret returned to the game. She tried to avoid the ball at all costs.

Gila had the ball and threw it at Sara, hitting her knees.

"Yes!" Gila shouted jubilantly.

"That's not nice," Kinneret admonished.

"Oh, yeah? And hurting someone in the stomach is nice?" Gila laughed.

Sharon caught the ball and quickly threw it at Ilana, hitting her on the arm. Ilana was out.

The ball was back in Gila's hands. She aimed for Miranda and missed. Miranda aimed at Kinneret, but Kinneret sidestepped it and ran away from the ball. Miranda ran after the ball and picked it up again.

"Why didn't you run after the ball?" Gila screamed. "Now we're going to lose because of you!"

Kinneret ignored her, concentrating on avoiding the ball. But then Gila passed the ball right to Kinneret who was standing not three feet away from Sharon.

Everyone screamed, "Get Sharon, Kinneret! Get Sharon!"

So much noise, Kinneret thought, wincing. She held the ball, feeling the rage inside her begin to take over. She pulled her arm back and catapulted the ball forward with a tremendous *WHOOSH*.

The ball caught Sharon between the shoulder blades, sending her sprawling across the gym floor.

"We won!" the cheer went up from the girls on Kinneret's team.

Kinneret stood stock-still. "I'm sorry," she said aloud, although no one was near enough to hear her. Another casualty. She had done it again. To a friend.

"I'm sorry," she repeated, feeling her head about to explode. She walked over to Sharon, who was crying.

"I'm sorry I hurt you," she said softly, "I never meant that you should be hurt."

"Well, control your strength," Sharon demanded between sobs.

I can't, Kinneret thought despondently, because it isn't strength, it's anger.

"You should be happy. YOU won the game," Dalia told Kinneret as they were changing from their gym pants into their skirts.

"I didn't win anything," Kinneret told her friend, sadness evident in her eyes. "I just made people hate me, more than ever. That's all I do. That's all I ever do. Even when I win."

Chapter 15

"What don't you understand, Kinneret?" asked Mrs. Braun, leaning over Kinneret's desk. She was in a hurry. It was almost time for afternoon recess, and she wanted to go over the math examples out loud with the class.

"How can two over two equal one?" Kinneret asked in a small voice. "If you take two cakes and divide them both in half, then you get four pieces of cake, and the answer is four, not one."

Mrs. Braun resisted a strong urge to laugh.

"I actually never thought of it that way. You know what?" Mrs. Braun said, looking at her watch, "I don't really have the time to explain right now. I'll speak to your resource room teacher and ask her to explain it to you. Okay?"

Kinneret, red-faced, nodded, clenching her teeth. She looked around her, wondering if anyone else had heard. Her head started throbbing again, around the temples.

But how could that be? Kinneret wondered. Whenever you divide a number by itself, the final number has to be bigger, not smaller.

They changed the rules again! The pounding in her head was getting stronger.

"One thing, girls, before we break for recess. The English book report that is due next week has to include a summary of the book and a diary entry by one of the characters describing how he or she feels when a problem arises."

Kinneret looked at the teacher's mouth intently. She didn't understand what the teacher wanted everyone to write in their diary. She didn't even have a diary. And what problem was the teacher talking about? She was sure her mother would help her solve it, if only she could find out.

"You can go outside for recess, now. Don't forget you have science with Mrs. Flaumen when you come back. She's taking over the next period because I have to leave early. Don't be late."

The class filed out to the playground.

Late for what? Kinneret thought as she joined the other children. Why don't teachers finish their sentences? Whenever I don't finish my sentence the teacher takes off points. Why don't they take off points for teachers who don't finish sentences?

Why do they always change the rules?

Chapter 16

"Calm down, girls. I know this is the last class of the day, but if you try to give me your attention, I'll try to make this science class as interesting as possible," Mrs. Flaumen chirped, as the students found their seats.

"Today we will learn about volcanoes and what makes them erupt." She smiled, pointing to the model on her desk. "First let's learn the parts of the volcano."

For half an hour, Mrs. Flaumen droned on about volcanoes. Kinneret tried taking notes, but got hopelessly confused when the teacher tried to explain about the lava coming out of the cone of the volcano "like ice cream out of a cone." Kinneret couldn't understand how an ice cream cone and the cone of a volcano were similar.

The cone of the volcano is just the *opposite* of an ice cream cone, she said to herself. The wide part is on the bottom and the smaller part is on the top. And ice cream is cold, and lava is hot, boiling hot. And, most important, ice cream never shoots out of a cone like lava does.

What is she talking about? Kinneret wondered, deciding she would borrow Dalia's notes, as usual.

"That's enough about volcanoes," Mrs. Flaumen finally concluded. "Now you have ten minutes. Each of you will find a partner. Then each pair will choose a topic for their science project, and let me know what it will be."

Kinneret followed Mrs. Flaumen's words intently. She saw girls approaching each other, and after a few moments, realized that she had to find a partner. She turned to Dalia.

"Wanna be partners?"

"Sorry, Kinneret, I just made up with Melissa that I would be her partner."

"Oh," Kinneret said, feeling a school-ache coming on.

"You don't mind, do you? It's just that I'm always with you, and I'd like to try being with someone else."

Kinneret felt as if she had been stabbed in the back. "That's okay," she said, avoiding Dalia's eyes. The throbbing in her head was gaining in strength. IT was happening. What she had always been afraid of. She was losing Dalia. Now she would be all alone. She would have no one.

Her mouth felt dry, but she turned to Debra.

"Can we be partners?" she asked.

"Sorry, Kinneret. I'm already Sharon's partner."

"Leah, can we be partners?"

"I'm already with Arielle."

"Cynthia, can you be my partner?" Kinneret asked, desperately.

"Gayla's my partner, already."

When there was no one left to ask, Kinneret sat down in her seat. Nobody wants to be with me because I'm dumb and can't help anybody with anything. Nobody likes me because I'm stupid.

And everybody knows now, because I don't have a partner.

Kinneret looked out toward the ocean and called the bird. The bird came. It flew into the classroom, glistening, dazzling, its eyes two bright moonbeams. The bird took her away on its strong graceful back, over the ocean, big as always, and beautiful.

Mrs. Flaumen walked around the classroom, happy to see that the girls were excitedly planning their projects. She reached Kinneret and looked at her. Kinneret's mouth was slightly open, and her head was tilted off to the left side. She looked like she was staring out the window, but Mrs. Flaumen saw that Kinneret's eyes were almost closed, as though she were in a trance.

"Kinneret?" Mrs. Flaumen said quietly.

Kinneret did not respond.

"Kinneret!" Mrs. Flaumen repeated, louder this time, placing her hand on Kinneret's shoulder.

Kinneret jumped, then pulled back. She looked at her teacher as though seeing her for the first time.

"Are you okay?" Mrs. Flaumen asked, concerned.

"Yes," Kinneret answered, suddenly feeling detached and terribly tired. The bird had vanished.

"Who's your partner?"

"I don't have one," Kinneret answered, her voice low and sad.

"We'll make you into a threesome then," Mrs. Flaumen declared.

I'll be a burden, and they'll resent me, Kinneret thought. Or maybe Dalia will take me because she'll feel she has to. I want her to be my friend without pitying me.

Aloud, she said, "It's okay. I can do a project by myself."

"Are you sure you want to?"

Kinneret nodded slowly.

"Have you thought about the topic of your project?"

Kinneret knew immediately what her project would be. "Birds," she said.

"That sounds interesting. You can put your coat on now and get ready to go."

Kinneret stood up.

"Girls, as soon as you tell me your topics you may line up by the door," the teacher told the rest of the class.

Everyone started shouting out their projects, anxious to leave.

Kinneret put her books into her knapsack and went to the coat hooks to get her coat. Dalia and Melissa were directly in front of her.

"Why are you so friendly with Kinneret?" she heard Melissa ask. Kinneret stood still, wanting to leave, but unable to move. "I just can't believe that you two are best friends. She's so dumb. How about being my best friend?"

"Come on, Melissa, we have to tell the teacher the topic of our project," she heard Dalia reply.

The two girls walked toward the teacher's desk.

Kinneret, feeling dizzy, grabbed her coat and leaned against the wall to keep from falling. Her breathing became quick and shallow. After a while, she regained her composure and lined up with the others. She could hear them excitedly planning out their science projects with their partners.

The class walked down to the main entrance, and Mrs. Flaumen held the heavy door open as the girls filed out.

Kinneret breathed in deeply as soon as the cold air hit her face. She felt a wetness and looked up. It was raining.

"Hurry to the buses, girls!" she heard Mrs. Flaumen call out.

Kinneret took off her hood and lifted her head up to the rain. With wet hair and soaking lashes she turned around and looked toward the ocean, marveling at the raging, foaming waves. She stretched her arms out and closed her eyes, feeling the drops hit her fingers and face, then slide down her cheeks and neck.

These are God's tears, she thought. God is crying.

She opened her eyes and smiled as she saw her classmates darting for the buses.

Kinneret remembered a day many months before when she had dared the rain and storm to be angrier then she. She looked now at the sea and at the raindrops, a little smile playing on her lips.

"You can't win me!" she whispered defiantly. "You can't."

Chapter 17

Mrs. Pfeiffer met Kinneret at the door and kissed her daughter's wet forehead.

"I wish you didn't feel the need to take your hood off every time it rains," she sighed.

"We got the King David test back today," Kinneret said, remembering that she had to have her test signed.

"Oh, I'm sure you did okay," her mother said, hoping to avoid embarrassing her daughter. She knew Kinneret had failed. She always failed.

Kinneret dropped her head, looking at her sneakers.

"I failed."

Mrs. Pfeiffer gently put a hand under her daughter's chin and lifted her face, so she could look into her lovely eyes.

"So what, Kinneret. I know you tried. Don't worry about the mark. You'll see. Soon things will get easier."

"I got a twenty-two, Ima," Kinneret lamented. "Only twenty-two. That's the highest I can get."

"That's not true, Kinneret. You can do well. We just have to find the right way to test you."

"Anyway, guess who's coming for dinner?" she added, trying to get Kinneret's mind off the test.

"Who?" Kinneret asked.

"Grandma and Grandpa."

Kinneret smiled, her face suddenly bright.

"Go change into some dry clothes, then you can help me make the salad."

Kinneret picked up her knapsack and headed for her room.

"E-et, E-et," Miri called, running over to Kinneret.

Kinneret scooped up her baby sister.

"Wet, wet," Miri said earnestly, looking at Kinneret.

"Yes, Miri, I am wet, and you will be wet, too," she laughed, tickling her sister under the chin. Miri giggled uncontrollably.

"You want to come with me while I get dry?"

"Yet, dy," Miri agreed, putting both her arms around Kinneret's neck.

"Not dy, silly, DRY," Kinneret corrected.

"Illy dy," Miri repeated, planting a wet kiss on her sister's cheek. Kinneret laughed.

"Could you peel all six of them, please?" Mrs. Pfeiffer asked Kinneret, after she had changed out of her wet clothes. Miri was sitting on Kinneret's lap at the kitchen table.

"Sure," Kinneret answered, grasping a cucumber in one hand and a peeler in the other.

"Hi, Ima," Meyer said as he walked into the kitchen, grabbed a peeled carrot, and jumped onto the counter.

"I got a hundred on my spelling test today, Ima."

"Very good, Meyer."

Kinneret hugged her baby sister and began peeling another cucumber.

"You know there's this kid in my class, he's so stupid, he can't spell hardly anything at all. Now he goes for help to this special room in school called the resource room. I think he must be retarded."

Kinneret dropped the cucumber and the peeler. A feeling of dread ran through her. She had never heard anyone actually say it before. But could it be? she thought. Am I retarded? She felt especially sorry for her mother. Ima's got a retarded child. Me. Then Kinneret looked at her baby sister. Pretty soon you'll be smarter than me, too. Like all the rest.

Mrs. Pfeiffer glanced sideways at Kinneret.

"Meyer, never say anything like that again, do you hear me?" she said loudly. "If a person has some difficulty in spelling, it does not make him retarded. Some of the presidents of the United States couldn't spell. Many, many great people today can't spell."

Meyer hadn't expected his mother's reaction.

"But, Ima," he said, defensively, "you should see this kid. He's really dumb. I mean, he goes to the resource room."

Mrs. Pfeiffer wanted to explain to her son about the resource room. But it was too late.

"SHUT UP Meyer! JUST SHUT UP!" Kinneret roared, feeling her rage breaking the surface. Her face felt red and hot.

Startled, Miri began to cry.

Kinneret calmed down when she heard her sister wailing. She felt drained of energy. She put her arms around Miri.

"Don't cry," she said, lowering her voice. "I'm sorry I scared you, sweetheart. I'm so sorry."

"Hey, did you hear what she said to me?" Meyer asked his mother. "Are you going to let her say that?" he demanded.

"Meyer," Mrs. Pfeiffer sighed deeply, "Grandma and Grandpa will be here soon. Please go help Ahuva set the table."

Meyer angrily jumped off the counter.

"It's not fair!" he grumbled, as he walked toward the living room. "SHE gets away with everything around here."

"He doesn't mean what he says, Kinneret," Mrs. Pfeiffer said, turning to her daughter. "He thinks you're smart, and he's right. He just doesn't know what a learning disability is."

"I don't have a learning disability," Kinneret insisted.

"Why don't you comb Miri's hair? I'll finish up in the kitchen," Mrs. Pfeiffer said, realizing this was not the time to argue.

Kinneret took Miri upstairs to put her hair up in a barrette. Just as she finished, the doorbell rang. Holding Miri, Kinneret ran to the front door.

"Grandma! Grandpa!" all the kids cried, eyeing the presents their grandparents were holding.

"You kids are looking great," their grandfather beamed.

The younger Mr. Pfeiffer came to the door and kissed his father. "Hello, Dad," he said.

"Oh, the kids are so glad you're here. Let's sit down for supper," Mrs. Pfeiffer suggested.

They all sat down to eat. Meyer refused to sit next to Kinneret. He was still angry with her.

"This soup is delicious," the older Mr. Pfeiffer said, complimenting his daughter-in-law.

"Oh, Marvin, we nearly forgot to give the kids the chocolates we brought," his wife, Elaine, exclaimed.

She went to the hall closet and took out five gift-wrapped boxes from a big plastic bag. She handed one to each of her grandchildren. Micah was the first to open his.

"Wow," he cried, astounded. In his hand he held an enormous chocolate kiss, the size of his father's fist.

The rest of the children opened their boxes as well.

"Put it away now, kids. You can eat the chocolate after supper," their father said.

The kids ran to put their chocolate away in their rooms.

"Micah!" Kinneret admonished, watching her brother take a big bite off the top of his chocolate kiss. "Abba said AFTER supper."

"I just wanted to see if it was real," he whispered to her, earnestly.

Kinneret smiled. "Well, is it?"

"And how!" he replied, grinning widely and showing a huge gap where his two front teeth used to be.

Kinneret returned to the table first.

"How's my sweet Kinneret doing?" Elaine Pfeiffer asked.

"I'm fine, Grandma," Kinneret answered.

"We're very proud of Kinneret. She's so helpful with Miri," Kinneret's mother declared.

Kinneret smiled, her face lighting up.

"How is she doing in school? On her tests?" her grandmother wanted to know.

Kinneret's smile withered.

"Oh, fine," her father answered casually. "She just got a test back today."

Kinneret grimaced.

"She got a hundred," he said to his mother, smiling.

"That's a Pfeiffer for you," Kinneret's grandfather said proudly.

Kinneret looked at her father, dumb struck.

"You know, Kinneret," the older Mrs. Pfeiffer continued, "at your age, grades are the most important thing. I want you to work hard and do well."

"Oh, Mom, there are things more important than tests," Kinneret's father protested.

"Not at her age. Keep up the good work, dear," Kinneret's grandmother said, smiling comfortably.

Kinneret nodded.

"How's the business, son?" Marvin Pfeiffer asked, as the rest of the kids returned to the table.

"It's doing fine, Dad. Thanks."

Mrs. Pfeiffer came to the table with the salad. "What did I miss while I was in the kitchen?"

"Nothing, dear. Nothing at all," Elaine Pfeiffer said.

Kinneret excused herself and ran to the bathroom and locked the door. She looked into the mirror, and ran her hands along the side of her eyes, nose, and mouth, then gazed at the reflection of her gray eyes, questioning, wondering.

She opened the faucet and washed her face with cold water, then turned back to the mirror and looked at her dripping face.

You can't tell by looking, she consoled her reflection. She remembered a jingle she had once heard: "Stupid is as stupid does." *Does,* she said to herself. That's me. She looked at herself with disdain. She was slow and inadequate in a world where acquiring knowledge quickly was the formula to success.

Long before the fifth grade, Kinneret had realized that many people befriended you or loved you based on what they thought you had achieved. That was the hardest lesson of all, learning to equate love with accomplishment. But tonight, for the first time, hearing her grandmother praise her for getting imaginary grades, this lesson struck home...hard.

Kinneret went back to the table, anxious for her grandparents to leave. She was very quiet, but with the other children so talkative, no one seemed to notice. Finally, after her grandparents left, Kinneret slipped into bed, lulled into sleep by the steady pitter-patter of rain.

She was walking through a pasture, the sunlight dancing on the grass. She was in a white nightgown, barefoot, holding a rich red lily in each hand, spinning around, smiling, her hair soft on her face.

Suddenly, the sky darkened, and Kinneret saw them: dark-hel-meted soldiers. They were everywhere, hiding behind the rocks that suddenly sprang from the ground.

Kinneret lifted both hands, dropping the lilies. She walked toward the soldiers barefoot, with her arms raised in surrender.

A soldier stood up. He was holding a spear three times her length. Kinneret eyed him silently and continued walking, facing him, her arms raised high. The soldier ignored her sign of submission and charged, running toward her, spear in hand.

She could hear the beating of his boots on the ground.

He was coming so fast! His spear would rip her in half! Aiiii!

Kinneret's eyes flew open. She was on her stomach. Both her hands, which were underneath her, had fallen asleep. She sat up, breathing heavily, beating both hands on her pillow.

When the pins and needles passed, she got up to look at Miri in her crib. She carried the sleeping baby out of her crib, kissing her gently, and placed her in her own bed, then lay down beside her. Sometimes the nightmares stayed away when Miri was in bed with her. The rhythmic breathing of the baby had a soothing effect on her, better than the rain, better even than the ocean.

She loves me, Kinneret thought as she put a protective arm over the baby. Miri loves me even if I can't accomplish anything. She loves me for nothing.

For nothing.

Chapter 18

"You explained the story you just read fabulously! Can you tell me what the main idea is?" Miriam Klein asked Kinneret.

Kinneret shrugged.

"Okay, maybe I wasn't too clear about what I wanted you to do. Why don't you explain to me what you think I just asked you to do," Miriam asked, pleasantly.

"I have to say what's the most uh...uh...the uum, uh, important thing is," Kinneret replied, frustrated with herself for being unable to express words that appeared so easily in her mind.

It was always so hard when she was asked to do a specific thing. Her mind couldn't or wouldn't help her get the words out.

"That's right, Kinneret. Now, can you tell me what the main idea is?"

"That, that the boy..." Kinneret looked up at the white ceiling. It helped her to concentrate when she saw only white. So many things happened in the story. What was she supposed to say? "The boy, he wanted to play outside like all his friends," she finally said.

"That's right," Miriam coaxed. "He wanted to play outside like all his friends instead of sitting in the principal's office, talking with the principal. But why was he in the principal's office?"

"Because he, uh, uh," Kinneret desperately sought the words for the answer that was so clear in her head. "He, uh, got into trouble. They said that he stole the lunch money, and they would check if it was true. They would, uh, kick him out from the school."

"Very good. And what was Fred afraid of?"

"His parents would be angry because they, they, they, *warned*," Kinneret pushed the word out, physically, "they warned him not to get into any trouble at his new school."

"So the main idea of the story would be that Fred was accused of taking lunch money. He was afraid of his parents, and the principal was questioning him."

Kinneret nodded.

"Now we're going to outline, with this marker, the sentences that tell us the main idea."

Kinneret nodded again. "Should I underline this?" Kinneret asked, holding the marker and pointing to a sentence.

"Yes, that's good."

"And this, too, to underline?"

Miriam nodded.

"And this?"

"What do you think, Kinneret?"

Kinneret shrugged.

"Try. What do you think?"

Kinneret looked up at her teacher's face, trying to decipher the answer. Miriam's face remained impassive.

"Yes, uh, no," Kinneret answered. "No," she repeated.

"But it IS right. Why did you change your mind?"

Kinneret shrugged again, feeling it was useless to explain that if she said yes, and she was wrong, then she was really wrong. If she said no, even though she thought it was right, then if it was wrong, SHE wasn't really wrong, because she knew the real right answer. It was all so complicated.

Kinneret underlined that sentence as well.

"Did Fred take the lunch money?" Miriam continued.

"No."

"Before we read the next part, what *should* Fred do?"

"Fred should try to...to...uh, um, prove to the principal that he didn't do it."

"What do you think Fred *will* do?"

"He'll run away," Kinneret replied, offhand.

Stunned for a moment, Miriam recovered quickly and offered an alternative suggestion. "You don't think maybe he'll talk to someone, maybe his parents or teachers, and try to explain?" she asked.

Kinneret shook her head angrily. "No," she said vehemently. "He shouldn't talk to anybody, because they won't believe him, and no one trusts him, because in his other school he stole, and they won't believe that in this school he decided not to ever steal again. That's how it goes. Once they think you are something or did something that's you forever!"

Miriam stared at the child in front of her. It was not so much what Kinneret had said, but the sudden realization that she was at war with the entire adult world.

How do you look into the eyes of a ten-year-old child and convince her to trust you, when she has already come to the realization that she cannot trust anyone? Miriam wondered.

"Well, we'll read the second part tomorrow. Let's put the story back in the drawer. Take out your math."

Kinneret stood up and took the math book out of her drawer. She liked the drawer, so neat and organized, with a pretty daisy on it. She was glad, though, that her name was still covered.

"Are grades the most important thing in life?" Kinneret asked Miriam as she sat down.

Miriam, surprised that Kinneret had actually initiated a question, thought for a moment. "No," she answered, raising her brows and bringing a finger to her chin. "There are many other things far more important than grades, like being a good, helpful person, and trying your best, and being honest. Why do you ask?"

"No reason," Kinneret replied defensively.

Miriam tried to change the subject. "How was Torah yesterday? Did the teacher ask you to name the Ten Commandments?"

"Yes."

"Did you answer the question?"

"No," Kinneret replied sullenly.

"Why didn't you, Kinneret?" Miriam asked gently. "When we reviewed it yesterday before class, you knew them all perfectly."

"No one else was raising her hand," Kinneret said, angry and uncomfortable because she felt she was being reproached.

"What's the difference if someone else is raising her hand or not?" Miriam asked, genuinely puzzled.

"If Esther and Ahuva and Dalia, none of them are raising their hands, then it can't be that my answer is right."

"But why?"

"It can't be that I know an answer they don't," Kinneret tried to explain.

"Why?"

"Because it can't," Kinneret repeated angrily, feeling a school-ache coming on. "Can we learn the math now?" Kinneret whispered, holding her head.

"Sure," Miriam agreed, noticing the way Kinneret's pupils had collapsed into little pinpoints of pain. "Are you okay?" she asked, concerned.

Kinneret nodded but didn't answer. She opened her math book to the lesson for the day.

Chapter 19

"You did the right thing, Miriam. Now will you please get off your knees so we can eat supper?" Yehudah called to his wife. Miriam was scrubbing the bottom of the kitchen cabinets.

"I'm coming, in a second," Miriam replied from somewhere inside the right bottom cabinet.

Yehudah sighed but waited patiently. Since he had come home he had watched his wife cook supper, do the laundry, and wash the floors. Now she was scrubbing the kitchen cabinets. All in under two hours.

Yehudah knew that this was how Miriam let off steam. Some people yelled; Miriam scrubbed. He was glad for that.

"Where are the cameras?" he asked in mock surprise. "Isn't this a Mr. Clean commercial?" he joked.

"I'm done," Miriam announced, emerging red-faced from within the kitchen cabinets. "And so are your jokes. Well done!"

"Very funny," Yehudah replied good-naturedly, taking the cleanser and rag out of her hands.

They washed and sat down to eat. Miriam brought out chicken and rice.

"How was your day today?" Miriam asked her husband, forcing a smile.

"Not great," Yehudah admitted. "I'd say it just about peaked when Professor Lailins started diagramming a geodesic dome and asked me for some equations. Unfortunately, I gave him the wrong equations, which as you may have already guessed, was quite embarrassing." Yehudah was talking rapidly, as he always did when he sensed that his wife was upset.

"Poor Yehudah," Miriam said in genuine sympathy. "I think you're one of the best people on the face of this planet. Everyone makes mistakes, believe me. It doesn't mean a thing."

"Well, maybe you're right." Yehudah saw he could no longer avoid the obvious. "Okay, who died?" he asked, grinning.

"Please, no more jokes," Miriam replied, anger flaring up in her usually calm brown eyes. She put down her fork. There was an uncomfortable silence at the table. Finally, Miriam spoke.

"You know how it is when you feel you need to help someone, but you also know you shouldn't get involved. Then, when you get involved, even though you did the right thing, you hate yourself for it?"

"Yeah," Yehudah, said encouragingly, thinking of about a dozen wise cracks he could have used for this occasion, but resolving not to.

"There's this girl, Kinneret. She just looks so helpless and lost."

"Maybe she belongs in a special school. Maybe a resource room isn't the answer to her problem," Yehudah suggested, then grimaced under Miriam's withering look.

"She improves every day," Miriam informed him. "I wish the teachers would improve at her rate. I don't get it. Are they thick, or just mean?"

"They just don't understand. They aren't used to it."

"Then why do they teach?" Miriam asked bitterly.

"I don't know," Yehudah replied, feeling as though he was being made to take the blame for the failures of the entire educational system.

Miriam wasn't going to let up. "If they would just try to understand her, things would be so different. We get cooperation from one or two teachers in the school, but that's all. I get the feeling that after a while even the few sensitive ones get tired of Kinneret's special needs. Don't they see it's not her fault?"

"She's a survivor," Yehudah ventured. "She's made it this far."

"But that's just the point," his wife replied. "People in deserts survive. Kids in school are supposed to flourish! What will she be like by the time she finishes high school? Every time she picks up her head to learn something, she gets punched in the face. How many more times until she stops lifting up her head altogether?"

"Aren't you getting a little melodramatic?" Yehudah asked.

"Melodramatic! Kinneret has an I.Q. of 125! How is it that no one thinks it's just a little bit bizarre for someone with an I.Q. of 125 to just SURVIVE in school?"

Yehudah whistled. "125, that's not bad."

Miriam realized she was making her point and continued full steam ahead. "Think what a success Kinneret would be if this was a language-less world. She'd be at the top of her class, not at the bottom. No one would be talking about putting her into a special school then," she told Yehudah.

"But this is the twentieth century, where language is crucial," Yehudah explained. "I don't mean to be cruel, but grunts and clicks, no matter how intelligent, don't count. Words count."

"Thank you for that update," Miriam replied tartly.

"Just doing my duty. Think nothing of it," Yehudah glibly retorted.

"Don't you see?" Miriam continued, "If she gets help now, then when she grows older, she'll really be something. She could put us both to shame."

"Well, I guess I'm just lucky you married me, what with my puny I.Q. and all. Maybe I could borrow a few points from her," Yehudah said, laughing at his own joke.

"That's not funny," Miriam said accusingly.

"I surrender," Yehudah declared, raising his arms and trying to stifle his laughter.

Chapter 20

"Kinneret, go to sleep already, it's 10 P.M.," Mrs. Pfeiffer said, irritated that all of her children were still up at this late hour.

"But my homework, Ima. We didn't finish it," Kinneret whined.

"We worked for over two hours tonight. That's enough. I'll write a note to the teacher."

Kinneret winced at the mention of the word "teacher." An involuntary shudder flowed through her body every time someone said it. She couldn't think of a single word in the English language she hated more.

"No, I'm not giving no more notes to the teacher. When I give her the notes, she always makes a face. I know what she thinks about me, and then the kids all see the notes at recess, because she leaves them on the desk."

"Kinneret, it's late," her mother pleaded. "You have to go to sleep."

"But, Ima, I have to do the homework," Kinneret said, a note of desperation in her voice.

Her mother could not resist. "So do what you can on your own, and then go to sleep," Mrs. Pfeiffer answered, exasperated, as she closed the door to Kinneret's room.

Kinneret went into the bathroom. She looked at her reflection in the mirror.

"I can't do the homework alone. I can't do any of it alone. Tell me what to do. It's too hard. It's always too hard," she said between clenched teeth, breathing hard.

As she left the bathroom, Kinneret heard whimpering noises from her sister Ahuva's room. She knocked softly, then opened the door. Ahuva was lying on her bed crying.

"What happened?" Kinneret asked.

"I failed my English test," Ahuva wailed.

"Don't be upset about failing that English test," Kinneret said, trying to console her sister. "It's not worth it."

Ahuva sat up and looked at Kinneret. "You don't understand. I never failed anything before in my whole life, and now I failed a test."

"I've failed tests plenty of times," Kinneret admitted, not knowing what else to say.

"But I'm not like you!" Ahuva cried. "Everyone expects me to do well. I always do well. I'm not used to failing."

"You don't ever get used to it," Kinneret countered, aware of something inside of her dying in that room, feeling frustrated because there was nothing she could do about it. "You cry after failing one test —" she said coldly, unable to finish her sentence.

"No one asked you to come in here anyway, so just get out!" Ahuva shouted.

Kinneret looked at her sister with pained eyes and silently left the room.

When she returned to her own room, she took out her Torah note-book and looked at the homework questions. For half an hour she worked, filling in answers she made up, answers which she knew had no relevance at all to the text. She filled up two pages, knowing she had a fairly good chance that Mrs. Rubenstein wouldn't call on her. If she did, she would have an answer — it just wouldn't be right.

"Kinneret?" a voice called.

"What?" Kinneret replied without looking up. Ahuva was stand-ing at the door.

"I was all upset. I'm sorry I yelled and everything."

"It doesn't matter. Forget it," Kinneret answered curtly, still look-ing into her notebook.

Ahuva wished Kinneret would look at her. She wished Kinneret would react one way or another — smile, scream, something.

"Well, good night," Ahuva said, frustrated.

"Good night," Kinneret replied distantly.

A few minutes after Ahuva had left the room, Kinneret changed into her pajamas, turned off the light, and got into bed. She tried to clear her mind of all thoughts.

Some days it hurt too much to think.

Chapter 21

Night.

Kinneret felt her pulse throbbing, its frantic pounding echoing in her neck and head, as she raced along the pavement. The back of her left hand swiftly swiped at her forehead to remove the sweat.

RUN! RUN!

She reached a lawn with hedges, staying low so she would not be seen. They were after her again. Two figures in the shadows. They were so quick. She knew she could not afford even one small mistake.

Kinneret's fear turned to terror. She just had to make it, had to get there — to the safe place. She was conscious of skimming the grass ever so lightly, of willing her feet to move forward. She crouched and waited for a moment. The two figures were close. Even from a distance they seemed to tower over her.

She felt her breath coming hard. She tried to stop heaving. QUIET! she told herself. Quiet.

The safe place. Which way? Kinneret looked out into the darkness at the unfamiliar terrain.

Which way? Which way?

I DON'T KNOW WHICH WAY TO RUN!

They're so close.

Kinneret looked far out into the darkness.

Run as fast as you can. Don't stop!

But they knew what she was thinking. And they were so quick. So close.

She prepared to run.

The shadow closest to her lunged.

Kinneret looked at her watch. 8:50 A.M. She hated this part of the morning, but it was always over quickly. She stood up, and, as silently as she could, left the classroom, certain that everyone was watching her leave.

She walked down the corridor on her own to the resource room. She had started walking there by herself three days before, after telling Miriam that she was sure she knew the way. She turned left, and then right, before going down two flights of stairs.

"So this is the last day before Chanukah vacation," Miriam smiled, greeting her at the door.

Kinneret nodded as she walked in.

"Do you have any plans?"

Kinneret raised her head. "For what?"

"Chanukah."

Kinneret nodded again. "We're going to the circus."

"What do you like the best about the circus?"

"The people who fly in the air and hold onto the stick, like a bar."

"What's the bar called? It starts with a *T.*"

Kinneret thought for a few moments, conjuring the word up to memory. "Trapeze," she blurted out.

"And what are the people who fly in the air with a trapeze called?"

Kinneret wrinkled her nose.

"It starts with an *A*," Miriam hinted.

"I forgot," Kinneret finally said, and felt at ease because she knew it was all right to forget here. She never needed to call the bird when she was in the resource room.

"I'll write down three words and you pick out the right one, okay?"

Kinneret nodded. Miriam took out a piece of paper and wrote down: "ACTOR ACTIVE ACROBAT."

Kinneret immediately pointed to "ACROBAT."

"That's right," Miriam smiled. "Do you want to be an acrobat when you grow up?"

Kinneret shook her head.

"What do you want to do?"

"I'm going to move far away from here, where no one knows me. I want to be a doctor."

"I think you'll make a great doctor, Kinneret."

"Do you think I'll stop mixing things up by then?" Kinneret asked painfully.

"I think, with a lot of work, you definitely can. Let's get the math."

Kinneret walked over to her drawer. "The cardboard that's covering my name is coming off," Kinneret said, ripping it off.

"I'm glad you decided to show your name," Miriam said, smiling.

"So am I," Kinneret sighed.

Chapter 22

SIX MONTHS LATER.

"Yes, but you have to agree that Kinneret is doing much better than before," Miriam told Mrs. Rubenstein as they were sitting in the teachers' room.

"There is no doubt, my dear, and for the past three or four months I have done as you suggested and tested her orally. You keep assuring me that she knows the work, but she is barely passing, and has received only one seventy during this time. And, let me remind you, all this *improvement* is with me reading out the questions to her!"

"But don't you see, Mrs. Rubenstein, her problem isn't reading the questions. It's understanding what is being said. If you just read the questions out loud to her it doesn't really help. The trick is to read the questions with the proper inflections so she understands what has to be emphasized."

"But I'm not an actor," Mrs. Rubenstein said indignantly. "I can't create melodrama when there is none."

"You're missing the point, I think," Miriam countered, aware that she had to walk on thin ice. "You need to explain the questions to her. Make sure she repeats the question in her own words. Only then can you be sure she understands."

"That takes time. I have an entire class to worry about. The last time I tested her, it was during my badly-needed break."

"She missed her recess, too," Miriam reminded her, tired of being diplomatic. "Maybe you can test her during your free periods," Miriam suggested, "or take her out of a different class for a half hour. I'm sure the principal will allow it," she assured Mrs. Rubenstein, having already checked.

"All right. The class takes the test before recess tomorrow. She can go over the test for that hour, and I'll test her orally, right after recess, before she goes to science class."

"Fabulous!" Miriam cheered. "Thank you."

"I only hope that child will eventually make something of herself."

"She will," Miriam answered. "If only you'd believe in her," she mumbled as she walked away.

Later that morning, Miriam was sitting with Kinneret in the resource room.

"I spoke to Mrs. Rubenstein. She'll give you the test orally after recess instead of science, *and* she'll explain the questions like we talked about."

"I can't," Kinneret said, her gray eyes clouding.

"Yes, you can."

"I'd rather fail than be tested like that. Who cares? It won't count anyway, because she'll give me the answers."

"It does count, Kinneret," Miriam explained. "We already talked about that. She's not giving you any answers. She'll just make sure you understand the questions, that's all.

"Give it one more try, Kinneret. Come on, we studied so hard for this test. You can do it. I know you can. You're a strong girl."

"No I'm not," Kinneret corrected. "I only manage because *it* stays with me."

"What stays with you?"

"Nothing," she replied quickly, realizing her mistake.

Miriam could feel Kinneret closing herself off, slipping away, but she tried to get through anyway.

"Is it a lucky charm?"

The bird. Miriam wanted to know about the bird, Kinneret thought in panic. NOBODY could ever be told about the bird. The bird needed to be kept safe. It needed to be kept a secret, a secret which only Kinneret could know. Otherwise it would die.

"It isn't anything," Kinneret repeated defensively, feeling violated. "Can we finish studying?"

"Yes, we'll study," Miriam agreed, realizing she was not going to get anywhere with her student. "And tomorrow after recess, you'll take the test."

Chapter 23

"What if I don't do well, Ima?" Kinneret asked her mother, who was sitting on the bed beside her.

"Go to sleep now. It's late. Don't worry so much, Kinneret. The important thing is that you studied. You've passed every single test you've taken in the past three months."

"But I don't do well. I just pass."

"Good night, sweetheart. You'll do just fine."

"My head hurts," Kinneret said, wanting her mother to stay near her just a little longer.

"It's because you're tired, Kinneret. Go to sleep."

Kinneret closed her eyes. Eventually she slept.

When she awoke, the clock read 2:16 A.M. She had dreamt of the soldiers again. She felt a drop of sweat trickle down the right side of her face near her eye. They would get her eventually, especially the soldier with the long spear. He had no mercy. He was going to kill her.

Kinneret stood up and turned to her sister, who was sleeping soundly in her crib. She walked over to the crib and held onto the bars.

"Miri, you gotta pray from now that you'll be nothing like me," she whispered desperately. "You've got to pray to be smart.

"That's the most important thing. And I'll pray for you, too. I'll ask God not to punish any more kids in our family, to let me be the last one to be like this. I promise I'll do that for you, Miri."

Kinneret glanced at her sleeping sister, suddenly feeling very tired. She went back to her bed, feeling a little better now. As though she had finally done something important.

As though she had saved a life.

Chapter 24

Kinneret sat in science class, waiting. She had been certain Mrs. Rubenstein would give her the test before class started. Now everyone would see her leaving...

Ten minutes later, Mrs. Rubenstein called Kinneret out of the classroom and walked with her down the hall to the teachers' room.

Kinneret concentrated on looking intently down at her sneakers. Although her school-aches came less frequently now, and were less severe, she felt a rising, steady pain in her temples.

"So you studied hard?" Mrs. Rubenstein inquired.

"Yes," Kinneret answered. Her study sessions with Miriam had instilled in Kinneret a new self-confidence which was slowly becoming evident in her improved grades. Nevertheless, at times like this, many of her fears and self-doubts returned.

"That's important. As a rule, those who study hard succeed," Mrs. Rubenstein intoned, feeling self-righteous.

"There are no rules," Kinneret wanted to say aloud to her teacher. She wanted to turn to her teacher, look her in the eye, and tell her that there was no logic or connection between studying and succeeding. It was purely random, arbitrary. It was a gift most kids got from God. The rest just didn't deserve it, for whatever reason.

They entered the teachers' room. Kinneret felt ill at ease. This room was the nest of the group she feared the most, teachers. At first she wanted to run away — to call the bird and make it take her away — but then she remembered that Miriam believed in her, and she felt strong.

Kinneret looked around, noticing two teachers lounging on a couple of chairs. They both looked up at Kinneret. She tried hard not to show her humiliation. They would KNOW now. They would see how different she was.

I won't call the bird. I'll get through this myself, Kinneret determined silently.

"Okay, Kinneret," Mrs. Rubenstein said, her hands folded across her chest. She was looking at Kinneret over the top of her glasses. "Who is the Kohen, the priest, allowed to marry?"

Kinneret tried to piece all the parts of the question together.

When her teacher saw she was still thinking, Mrs. Rubenstein added, "Explain what I have asked of you."

"To say who the priest can marry."

"That's right," Mrs. Rubenstein replied, wondering why she had to bother with this. Kinneret obviously understood the questions. This whole learning-problem thing was overemphasized, in her opinion.

"Can you tell me the answer?"

"I only know who the priest CAN'T marry," Kinneret said with worried, nervous eyes.

"The priest can marry anyone who is not on the 'can't marry' list. That would be everyone except — what four groups of women?"

Kinneret looked at her teacher, stupefied by the sequence of words she had just heard, unable to decipher a meaning.

"All right, Kinneret," Mrs. Rubenstein sighed. "Tell me who the Kohen can't marry."

Kinneret rattled off the answers easily.

"Compare the commandment of honoring your parents with shooing away the mother bird when you want to take the chicks. Tell me what you have to do."

"Say what's the same."

"And what else?"

Kinneret shrugged her shoulders, frustrated.

"To compare means to say what's the same and also what the difference is between two things," the teacher explained.

"The same is that you get the reward for long life when you do these commandments, and the difference is that one is easy and one is hard."

"Fine. Now, what is the name of the holiday when the Jews received the Torah?"

Kinneret knew that answer. It was easy. But what was its name again? How was it called? How could she dig it out of her memory?

"It's the holiday that the Jews got ready for three days," she said, hoping the teacher would give her a hint once she saw she knew what it was. When Mrs. Rubenstein just looked at her, she continued, more desperately, "And we stay up all night and learn, and it's after Pesach."

"I know you know what it's about, Kinneret, but I need the name. What's its name?" Mrs. Rubenstein repeated.

Why were the exact names always so important?

"Okay. Let's go on. What are the dates of the following holidays: Rosh Hashana, Pesach, Sukkot and Shavuot?"

"Shavuot," Kinneret called out, recognizing the word she had been unable to recall. "That's when the Jews received the Torah," she said, knowing it was too late.

"What are the dates?" Mrs. Rubenstein repeated.

Kinneret knew them all. She had gone over them with Miriam many times. Miriam showed her how to remember. She had to think carefully and concentrate so she wouldn't say Sivan instead of Nissan.

"Pesach is on fifteenth of" — Kinneret paused for a moment, fighting to get the right word out — "Nissan." It was right. She knew she had said it right.

Twenty minutes later, Mrs. Rubenstein released Kinneret, and Kinneret, unaided, returned to class.

Chapter 25

"We're getting the Torah tests back today. Mrs. Rubenstein promised us," Dalia whispered excitedly to Kinneret one morning before recess.

Kinneret looked out toward the ocean. It was high tide and the water looked quiet and peaceful.

"After I hand back your tests, you may go for recess. Sara, Nina, Melissa, Rivka, Mindy, Kinneret, Miranda...," Mrs. Rubenstein called.

Kinneret began a slow steady walk toward her teacher. It was the same path she had taken a hundred times, and one she loathed.

The pain in the back of her head was already starting. Kinneret looked up at her teacher's face. She cringed, expecting a look of disapproval — or worse, disdain — from Mrs. Rubenstein.

Mrs. Rubenstein held Kinneret's test in her right hand. She looked up briefly and said, "Good job."

Kinneret stood numbly, holding her test paper. Her school-ache was steadily expanding, pressing against the back of her eyes. The danger signals in her head were flashing. Her teacher had said something to Kinneret that just didn't make any sense to her.

"Kinneret, what did you get?" Dalia asked, bouncing over to her.

Kinneret opened up her test paper so she could see her grade. She read it and felt nothing. It was as if the mark was given to someone outside of her, someone she did not recognize.

She drew the paper close to her chest, ashamed that Dalia should see her test paper, the paper without a single word written except the mark, because she had taken the test orally.

"It's only a stupid test, Dalia. It's not important," Kinneret replied uneasily, gulping hard. "I got an eighty," she lied.

Dalia was not so easily put off. "Come on, Kinneret. If Mrs. Rubenstein said 'good job' you must have done something special. Let's compare answers," Dalia suggested, opening up her hand.

But all Kinneret could think was, If Dalia sees my test paper, she'll think I'm a freak. She'll never understand.

"Did I hear right?" Gila asked, coming over to the two girls. "Mrs. Rubenstein actually said 'good job'? This I have to see." She reached out to take the test paper, but Kinneret pulled it even closer to her chest.

"It's none of your business," Kinneret told her, more anger in her voice than she had intended.

"I'll bet Mrs. Rubenstein made a mistake," Gila teased. "She probably meant, 'lousy job,' which for *you* is a 'good job'."

"Kinneret, come on, let me see," Dalia cut in, playfully trying to take the paper out of Kinneret's hands.

Panicking, Kinneret clutched the paper tighter and pulled back. She heard the sound of ripping paper and saw a torn piece of her test paper in Dalia's hands.

"Sorry, Kinneret," Dalia grinned sheepishly. "But you tore the paper, not me."

Dalia was about to give the torn paper back when another girl yelled, "Wow, look what it says!"

All eyes were immediately riveted to the ripped paper.

"Ninety-three! Kinneret, that's great!" Dalia screamed out. "I'll never figure you out, Kinneret. Why did you say you got an eighty?"

Debra, Sharon, and Sara came over. Kinneret was aware they were talking about her and her grade, but she couldn't understand what they were saying. There was too much noise in the class.

"Wow, Kinneret got a ninety-three."

"That's a great mark."

"I never knew Kinneret got those kind of marks."

Kinneret crumpled up her blank test paper and hastily stuffed it into her skirt pocket. Then she took the jagged paper with the grade out of Dalia's hand and ran out of the room.

She saw a second-grader leaving the resource room and Miriam about to lock up.

"Miriam!" she called aloud. "Miriam!"

Miriam dropped the keys she held in her hand.

"Kinneret, what's the matter?" she asked, startled.

"Miriam," Kinneret said again, breathless, as she reached her teacher.

She pulled the crumpled test out of her skirt pocket, feeling so out of breath that she could not speak. She handed the paper to Miriam.

Oh no, Miriam thought, as she smoothed out the crumpled paper and saw the blank page. The teacher didn't even give her a grade.

"Don't worry about it, Kinneret. I'm proud of you. You tried hard. Although I really don't understand —"

"Wasn't ninety-three good enough?" Kinneret interrupted, wondering if perhaps everyone had read the mark wrong. Perhaps she had received a thirty-nine?

Kinneret felt her palms begin to sweat and looked down at her hands, suddenly realizing that the grade was on the torn piece of paper still in her hand. She opened her palm and held up her grade for Miriam to see.

"Oh, Kinneret," Miriam exclaimed, both embarrassed at her lack of faith in her pupil and ecstatic about Kinneret's achievement. Instinctively she reached down and hugged Kinneret.

Kinneret began to laugh, a clear, strong, ringing laugh, as she returned her teacher's hug.

Miriam couldn't help but notice that for the first time, Kinneret did not pull away.

"Thank you," Kinneret said, looking up at Miriam.

"Thank yourself," Miriam answered. "You'd better run along to your classroom. You aren't supposed to be here now," she added in mock anger as she tweaked Kinneret's nose.

Later, Miriam would remember that exact moment as the turning point in her career. It was then that she realized that all the effort she had put into teaching Kinneret had been worth it. It was then she *knew* that she had picked the right profession.

As she locked the resource room, Miriam smiled. She could hardly wait to tell her husband about this wonderful day.

Chapter 26

"Did you get the test back?" Kinneret's mother asked the moment she got home.

Kinneret nodded, reaching into her knapsack for the test paper. She clutched it and, for some reason, started to cry. She cried and cried and couldn't stop, her shoulders heaving silently. She felt as though a terrible weight had been lifted from her, as though the curse was gone. But this freedom only lasted a moment.

"Kinneret, it isn't worth it. You did your best," Mrs. Pfeiffer said, stroking her daughter's hair. "Please don't cry."

Kinneret handed handed the test paper to her mother. She had taped the mark back onto her paper.

Mrs. Pfeiffer opened the test paper.

"A ninety-three!" she shouted, stupefied. "Kinneret, that's amazing. That's terrific!

"Michael, look at Kinneret's test!" Mrs. Pfeiffer called out to her husband.

Mr. Pfeiffer came to the door and picked up Kinneret's test paper.

"Kinneret, this is really great!" he enthusiastically complimented her.

But Kinneret could not stop crying. It suddenly dawned on her that she had never gotten a ninety-three before, and she didn't know if she could ever do it again.

"This calls for a celebration. Let's order pizza for supper," Mr. Pfeiffer suggested.

An hour later the doorbell rang. Meyer and Micah ran to the door, shouting, "Pizza's here!"

The smell of pizza drew the family to the dining room.

"Yum, pizza!" Micah cried.

"Did you order a slice with green peppers?" Ahuva asked.

"Kinneret, we're so proud of you," Mrs. Pfeiffer beamed, as she helped her to a slice.

"Everyone makes such a big deal when Kinneret gets a ninety-three," Meyer whined. "I've gotten a hundred plenty of times, and we never ordered pizza!"

Everyone fell silent. Mr. and Mrs. Pfeiffer exchanged looks, realizing their mistake.

Kinneret put her slice of pizza down and quietly said, "He's right. And anyway, it's just a fluke. I couldn't do it again in a million years, no matter how hard I tried."

"That's not true," her father insisted. "If you did it once, you can do it again — and again! The important thing is not the ninety-three but the fact that you knew the work, and the teacher knew you knew it."

Kinneret looked from her father to her mother and saw their hopeful, concerned faces. She tried hard to feel good about herself, as good as she had felt when she first saw her grade. But what if it *is* a fluke? she kept thinking. What will everyone say when I bring home a twenty-two next time?

Chapter 27

Mrs. Pfeiffer tiptoed into Kinneret's room to check on her two sleeping daughters before she went to bed. She looked at Kinneret and sighed contentedly. Her daughter's face looked so peaceful for a change. Just then, Kinneret laughed in her sleep. The laugh was so free that it sounded like a little child's laugh. It reminded Mrs. Pfeiffer of the time she had taken the children to the zoo, when they were very small. Only Kinneret had wanted to go on the camel ride. She sat alone atop the camel, looking so small and fragile. Mrs. Pfeiffer had been sure that her daughter would fall off any minute.

After the ride, Kinneret had run toward her mother, laughing and screaming, "I did it, Ima! I did it all by myself!"

Kinneret had been so proud and eager.

It was that laugh that Mrs. Pfeiffer heard now.

She was happy for her daughter, and happier still that Kinneret had Miriam and the resource room to help her feel good about herself.

But, at the same time, she couldn't help being angry — angry at the school that had waited so long to help Kinneret, and angry at herself for not pushing harder to have such help made available to her daughter.

But beyond the happiness and the anger lay apprehension. The feeling that the battle had just begun, and that there was still such a long, long way to go.

"It's all worth it," Mrs. Pfeiffer whispered to her sleeping daughter, "and things will only get better from now on. I know they will," she smiled, stroking Kinneret's hair.

Chapter 28

Midnight.

Kinneret felt her pulse throbbing, its frantic pounding echoing in her neck and head, as she raced along the pavement. The back of her left hand swiftly swiped at her forehead to remove the sweat.

RUN! RUN!

She reached a lawn with hedges, staying low so she would not be seen. They were after her again. Two figures in the shadows. They were so quick. She knew she could not afford even one small mistake. Kinneret's fear turned into terror. She just had to make it, had to get there — to the safe place. She was conscious of skimming the grass ever so lightly, of willing her feet to move forward. She crouched and waited for a moment. The two figures were close. Even from a distance they seemed to tower over her.

She felt her breath coming hard. She tried to stop heaving.

The safe place. Which way? Kinneret looked out into the darkness at the unfamiliar terrain.

Which way? Which way?

I DON'T KNOW WHICH WAY TO RUN!

They're so close.

Kinneret looked far out into the darkness.

Run as fast as you can. Don't stop! Find the safe place. Don't stop!

But they knew what she was thinking. And they were so quick.

So close.

She ran again, feeling her breath coming hard.

Then she saw it, a door with a handle. She had to get inside. She had to run just a little faster. Twenty feet and she would make it to the door. Kinneret raced, crying out from the sheer pain of her exertion.

They were still behind her.

So close.

Kinneret bounded for the door, pulled it open, then slammed it shut behind her, trembling. She turned around and looked at her surroundings. She saw a room, bright and full of colors. There were balloons everywhere, and on one wall there were happy words that were pleasant for the eye to read.

She saw a wall full of drawings by small children, and a chest of drawers with a daisy on each drawer. And on each drawer there was a name. Kinneret recognized her name, and smiled. She opened the drawer, and out flew the bird, fluttering and gliding around the room. It was soft and strong and beautiful. For an instant she thought to call it, to bring it to her, but then she realized she didn't need it.

Not now.

This was the safe place.

At last.

She looked up and saw a smiling, dark-haired young woman, beckoning her. Kinneret walked toward those open arms, laughing...